Alison broke the kiss by tossing her head and struggled to sit up. "Nic, don't be silly. Why are you acting like this? Who says I'm an ice maiden?"

"Everyone," Nic replied. "All the guys you won't make out with, won't even date twice. But Nic's going to thaw the ice maiden tonight. Yes, sir!"

Alison struggled harder. But the more she fought the more Nic seemed to enjoy it. "Come on, baby, fight! It makes the prize that much sweeter."

"Nic, let me up! Let's go back to the party."

We'll go back," he said, "but not until I've won my hundred-dollar bet."

His words shocked Alison into immobility. . . .

ODD ONE OUT

Lou Kassem

FAWCETT JUNIPER • NEW YORK

RLI: $\dfrac{\text{VL 5 \& up}}{\text{IL 6 \& up}}$

A Fawcett Juniper Book
Published by Ballantine Books
Copyright © 1993 by Lou Kassem

All rights reserved under International and Pan-American
Copyright Conventions. Published in the United States of
America by Ballantine Books, a division of Random
House, Inc., New York, and simultaneously in Canada by
Random House of Canada Limited, Toronto.

Library of Congress Catalog Card Number: 93-90541

ISBN 0-449-70432-7

Manufactured in the United States of America

First Edition: January 1994

This book is dedicated to the Tennessee Mountain Writers. You took the odd one in. Many thanks from your Virginia connection.

Chapter
One

"Thanks for the ride, Mrs. Trevor." Alison stepped from the air-conditioned car into the August heat. She could almost feel her hair frizzing.

"Thank you for being an aide at Meadowbrook. The old folks simply adored you! I'm glad your mother suggested you volunteer."

"My pleasure."

"See you next summer," Mrs. Trevor called as Alison shut the door and the car purred away.

You just might, Alison thought. It's one of the few things that Mother has talked me into that's worked out. Which brought her abruptly back to the present problem . . .

"It's crunch time," she said as she walked slowly up the tree-lined drive leading to the two-story Georgian brick house that had always been her home.

Looking up at the house, she smiled. It seemed to welcome her every time. When she was little she'd imagined the house to be a face. A warm, red-brick face. The lower windows were the mouth and the top windows were the sparkling eyes, which always watched for her safe return.

"Alison! Over here! Gee, I thought you'd never get back. I've been waiting for hours. Well, not exactly hours . . . minutes really. Seemed like hours. Guess what? I made it! I got my invitation in today's mail!"

The words and the girl tumbled out from under the shade of a massive oak. Deek Thomas was aglow with happiness. It radiated from every pore—from the top of her short, curly hair to the soles of her never-still feet. Darleen Kathryn Thomas (Deek, for short) wasn't beautiful, but her bouncing joy for life made her attractive and fun to be around. She was Alison's best friend.

"Slow down, Deek. You'll have a stroke in this heat."

"Oh, pooh! How can you be so calm?" Deek exclaimed, pulling Alison into the deep shade and down on a bench. "I know you got yours today, too."

"How do you know? How can you be so sure I'm one of the select few chosen to be one of Athena's Maidens?"

"Don't be silly. With your looks and your brains? You were a shoo-in."

Not to mention that both of my older sisters were Maidens, Alison added silently.

"Listen to this," Deek continued, waving an engraved card in front of Alison. " 'Pallas Athena and her Maidens request the pleasure of your company at their weekend house party on Drifter's Island, Friday, September first to Sunday, September third. RSVP.' It's engraved in gold! Isn't that radical?''

Deek's joy was infectious. Alison smiled, in spite of the niggling doubt in the back of her mind. ''Totally awesome. The Maidens always do things right. And I'm glad you were invited, although I was certain you would be. After all, you're a VIP at Chandler High—captain of our tennis team, a cheerleader, and a varsity guard on our basketball team. Athena's Maidens select only the best.''

Deek's freckled face flushed at the compliment. ''I wish I'd been so sure. I've been on needles and pins all summer.''

''I've never seen you look worried. You never said anything.'' Alison was a little put out that her best friend hadn't confided in her.

''Oh, I hid it pretty well,'' Deek said. Then seeing Alison's hurt expression, she added hastily, ''I thought you'd think I was silly. Besides, I didn't want to jinx my chances. Like, you know, a wish. But it's the most important thing that ever happened to me. And now that it really happened, I have a problem.''

''What problem? Can I help?''

''It's my folks. You know how old-fashioned they are. A weekend party with boys and girls? No way! I know they won't let me go. And I'll just up and die if I can't be a Maiden!''

''What can I do?''

''Get your mom to call mine and explain how innocent it is. How we'll be well chaperoned and all. My mother respects yours, and I know she'll listen to her.''

"Well chaperoned? By the Kanes? That's like setting a fox to guard the henhouse," Alison said, laughing. The Kanes were laid-back parents, notably indulgent of their daughter's activities.

Deek giggled, too. "You know what I mean," she said, sobering. "She doesn't have to know who all will chaperon. Besides, I can take care of myself, even if they don't think so. Will you do it, Alison?"

"Yes," Alison answered promptly. "Only it might be a bit awkward. I'm not sure I'm going to accept."

"Say what?"

"I haven't decided yet."

"Why not?"

"I don't know. My mother expects it. My sisters expect it. Even you think I should be overjoyed. And I'm not. Somehow it feels like a loss of my freedom . . . or something."

A rare frown creased Deek's brow. "You mean because everyone expects you to do it, you don't want to?"

"No, it isn't that, exactly," Alison said. "I can't quite explain it. The Maidens are so exclusive. Only eight senior girls and eight juniors. They do everything together. Dress alike. Think alike. Are leaders in everything. Or, if they aren't, the Sons of Apollo are. The Greeks practically run everything at Chandler. No one else has a chance."

"What's wrong with that? The Greeks are selected *after* they become leaders. And if it wasn't exclusive, it wouldn't be any fun to belong. Besides, both clubs do a lot of good things—clean-up campaigns, fund-raisers for school events, charity drives—all sorts of community work."

"I know. I didn't say they were altogether wrong. After all, these are people I've known most of my life. I just don't know if the Maidens are for me."

"It won't be the same unless you join," Deek said mournfully. "We'll never have time together. The Maidens are so busy."

"That's part of what I mean!" Alison said, her gray eyes flashing. "You only have time for each other. My gosh, Deek, there are two thousand students at Chandler. Look what you're missing."

"No one has time to be friends with two thousand people," Deek said practically. "Better a few good friends than a whole bunch of acquaintances."

Alison sighed. "I guess you're right. Maybe I'm just being stubborn."

"No, you're only being Alison," Deek said, laughing. "Totally cool, sophisticated, confident Alison. You always look before you leap. Not like old mud puddle Thomas here."

"Couldn't you just for once be a doubting Thomas?"

"Not this time. I really want *us* to be Athena's Maidens."

"Okay, okay. I'll think about it some more. Anyway, I'll ask Mother for you. Want to go in and do it now?"

Glancing at her watch, Deek said, "No, it's almost suppertime. Your mom's probably busy anyway. I'd better get home. Will you ask her tonight? I want to send in my reply."

"Sure. I'll call you later."

"Please think over your own answer, too," Deek called, jumping on her bike and pedaling furiously down the drive. "I'm late. Mom will be worried."

"Slow down, Deek," Alison called, but it was too late. Deek had already disappeared around the corner.

"I'm home," she called, letting herself into the air-conditioned comfort of the house with a sigh of relief.

"In here," Mrs. Grey answered from the den.

Mrs. Grey, a smartly dressed, trim, fifty-four-year-old woman who didn't look her age, smiled as Alison came into the room. "How was your last day at Meadowbrook?"

"Fine. I'll miss those folks. They're really sweet."

"I told you you'd enjoy them," Mrs. Grey said complacently. "I suppose Deek found you. She was bubbling over about her invitation."

"Yes, she was waiting for me under the oaks."

"Well, I tried to get her to wait in here out of the heat, but she couldn't sit still," Mrs. Grey said. "I'm sure you're happy she was asked to join."

"If that's what she wants. What's for dinner?"

Mrs. Grey looked at her sharply, but only said, "How about some tuna salad and tomatoes? I have strawberries for dessert. Your father won't be home for dinner."

"Sounds fine. I'll go up and change. I'll come back down and help."

"No need. Everything's almost ready. Twenty minutes?"

"Okay."

Upstairs, Alison took off the blue and white aide's uniform and put on shorts and a T-shirt. Sitting at the dressing table, she gave her hair a vigorous brushing until it lay smooth and shiny as a raven's wing on her shoulders.

Her reflection stared back at her in the oval mirror. She studied herself carefully: High brow, covered somewhat by her swept-back bangs; thick, arched eyebrows; long, curly eyelashes protecting the smoky gray eyes that everyone said changed color with her clothing or her moods—from gray to violet, or green to blue; high, prominent cheekbones (probably an Indian in her ancestry somewhere—wouldn't her mother love that!); an ordinary nose, not too long or too short; even, white teeth (thanks to two awful years in braces). Not bad, she decided. Even her chipmunk cheeks had disappeared along with the pudgy baby fat, just as her mother had said they would.

Alison blew out her cheeks, trying to capture how she'd looked in the ninth grade. Yuck! It was worth all the sacrifices—no candy bars, no hot fudge sundaes, no between-meal snacks of any kind for a whole year. Forcing herself to exercise by joining the swim team had been a blessing in disguise. She'd really enjoyed it.

So . . . her looks were okay. She didn't have zits, crooked teeth, blubbery fat or a wart on the end of her nose. She even had as good a figure as either of her older sisters. But in spite of all that, what Deek said wasn't true. She wasn't sophisticated or sure of herself. Maybe she looked that way but she certainly didn't feel that way.

Sighing, Alison picked up her unopened invitation and read the envelope aloud. "Ms. Alison Grey, 1017 Forest Hills Drive, Chandlersville, Virginia, 28601." She tossed it aside, unopened. "Be happy," she admonished her reflection. "It's your junior year. The year the cream rises to the top. You've just received notice that you're the cream. Only two things are important at Chandler: membership in the Maidens and a date for every function. You have one and, just possibly, the other. Why the long face, doofus?"

There was no answer from her reflection, but the thought of Nic Chandler did cause her eyes to glow with a special warmth. "Why, Alison, I do believe you're falling for that young man," she said mockingly, shifting her gaze to a snapshot on her dresser.

Nic. Big, bronze, blond, blue-eyed Nic Chandler. So handsome he didn't seem real. Nic, who had returned to Chandler High last year after years in military schools. He had taken the school by storm, not only with his good looks and family position (the Chandlers of Chandlersville), but by his abilities as well. This year he would be the quarterback of the football team, president of the senior class, and president of the Sons of Apollo. Every girl in school had a crush on him. And he'd certainly tried to satisfy all of them. Alison had not been one of the crowd that raced around the halls simply to catch a glimpse of him. Yet without any conscious effort on her part, three weeks ago Nic had started asking her out. . . .

"Alison! Al-i-son!" The impatient voice of her mother broke into her reverie.

"Coming."

"Alison, answer the phone! It's Nic. I've called you a half dozen times," Mrs. Grey said from the foot of the stairs.

"Sorry. I was—uh—thinking," Alison said, picking up the hall phone.

"Hi." Nic's deep voice rumbled at her. "Coach let us out of practice early because of the heat. Thought I'd call and see if you had plans for tonight."

"Nothing special."

"Want to double with Rob and Lucy for a Showtimer play in Rippley?"

Alison didn't particularly like Rob Warren, who had been Chandler's number-one jock until Nic came along. But he and Nic were best friends. "Sure," she replied, thinking Rob would be busy with Lucy, so she wouldn't see much of him. "What's playing?"

"*The Importance of Being Earnest.* Have you seen it?"

"We read the play in English but I haven't seen it performed. I'd love to go."

"Great. Pick you up at seven?"

"I'll be ready."

"Anything exciting happen today?"

"Nothing much. I worked out at the pool and went to Meadowbrook for the last time."

There was a small silence. "Have you checked your mail?" Nic asked.

"Oh! Oh, that. Yes, I received my invitation."

Nic laughed delightedly. "You really are cool, Alison. A real ice maiden. I wish Carol Hardy could have heard you."

Alison was embarrassed. "Oh, Nic, I didn't mean it the way it sounded. Of course the invitation is important." It wouldn't do to get on the wrong side of Carol Hardy. Besides being Athena this year, Carol was editor-in-chief of the yearbook and president of the student council, a beautiful and aggressive girl. Alison had crossed swords with her in student council—and lost.

Nic was still chuckling.

"Don't start trouble, Nic," Alison said sharply.

"No sweat, Snowflake. My lips are sealed. Just send in your acceptance. This party is going to be a real bash. We wouldn't want to miss it, would we?"

The "we" sent a little shiver of pleasure through Alison. "Certainly not."

"Good. See ya at seven. Bye."

Alison hung up and was stricken with a moment of panic. Had she promised she would join? No, not really. She'd only said she didn't want to miss the party. She could still change her mind.

"Alison, dinner's ready."

"I'll have to eat in a hurry," Alison said, joining her mother in the breakfast nook. "Nic's taking me to a play in Rippley."

"That's nice. Nic thinks of a lot of nice things for you to do, doesn't he?"

"Yes, he's different from most guys around here. He can actually carry on a conversation about something besides sports."

"Nic's had advantages most of them haven't. You shouldn't be so critical, dear."

"I'm not being critical. Just stating a fact," Alison said, bristling. What she thought silently was that Nic was different in another important way. In spite of his reputation, he didn't think because he took you out once or twice he owned you body and soul. Especially body.

"Well, I'm glad you've finally found someone who interests you. You don't stay at home nearly as much as you used to," Mrs. Grey said. Then, seeing the look in Alison's eyes, she added, "Not that you were a wallflower. It's just that you hardly ever dated a boy more than once. Like Kenny Maxton. Elsa told me he called you a half dozen times and you refused."

"He was one of the persistent ones. Most guys don't call back. I'm sorry if I hurt his ego."

"Well, there's more to life than books, swimming, and Deek. Not that I have anything against any of them. But these are the best years of your life. You shouldn't waste them."

Alison swallowed the retort on the tip of her tongue. No use getting in a fight with her mother tonight, especially if she needed a favor. She filled her mouth with tuna salad and chewed.

Parents were exasperating! You never seemed to have the right kind. Her mother wanted her to date—anyone, anytime, anywhere. Deek's mom wouldn't let her date—not without running an FBI check on the guy and the event. Better ask now, before she said something stupid. "Mother, would you do me a favor?"

"If I can, certainly. What is it?"

"Would you call Mrs. Thomas and tell her that the house party will be well chaperoned? Deek's parents are very protective. They might balk at the idea of a mixed house party."

"How quaint! We had mixed house parties even when I was a girl. My mother trusted me, just as I trust you. Yes, I'll call Mrs. Thomas and explain everything. Where is the party this year?"

"Drifter's Island. The Kanes' cabin."

"Oh. Well, I'm sure Deek is a sensible girl. I'll call tomorrow."

"Thanks. Deek would die if she had to refuse."

"I must say you don't seem too enthused," Mrs. Grey said. "Of course, you were almost certain to be invited. But it isn't good form to show your position so plainly."

"And just what is my position?" Alison inquired.

"Don't be coy and sarcastic with me, Alison. You know very well that our social credentials are impeccable. The Greys are an old, established family. Your father is president of his own company. I'm quite active in civic affairs. Your sisters were socially prominent and were both Maidens. That, my dear daughter, is your position."

"Everything you said is true," Alison said coldly. "You enumerated the positions of everyone else in our family. You said not one word about me! Am I only a reflection of everyone else? What happened to me—Alison Grey? I'm not sure I want to follow in Lisa and Ellen's well-trodden path. I may just want to find my own!"

"No one said you couldn't," her mother snapped. "You haven't had time to establish yourself. And so, yes, you are a reflection of your family. It's nothing to be ashamed of, either!"

"Just don't push me into the same mold. Sometimes I don't fit!"

"No one's pushing you. Just because I want you to date like other girls and join the best clubs, doesn't mean I'm pushing. Mothers are supposed to look after their children's best interests." She was close to tears.

It always ends this way, Alison thought as she got up and put her arms around her mother. "I'm sorry, Mom. I guess I'm just cranky with the heat."

Mrs. Grey dabbed at her eyes. "I don't know why we get into these silly discussions. You run along and get dressed for the play. I'll wash up."

"Okay. I'll call Deek first and tell her you'll call her mom tomorrow. Right?"

"Tomorrow morning."

Alison went upstairs and phoned Deek. "Mom says first thing tomorrow. And that isn't all. Guess what? Nic's taking me to a play tonight."

"Wow! Let's see, that makes a tennis date, a picnic, a concert, two movies, and a play!"

"Who's counting? Now you sound like my mother."

"No way! I can't help noticing, though. Has he put a move on you yet?"

Alison lowered her voice. "He hasn't even tried to kiss me. He's just fun to be with. I think his reputation was a jealous rumor."

"Or wishful imagination," Deek said with a giggle. "Have fun."

"We're doubling with Rob and Lucy."

"Oh, boy! That's one rep we know is true."

"Rob's or Lucy's?"

"Both, I guess."

"I hope the octopus has all eight hands busy with Lucy," Alison retorted. "The show in the backseat may be better than the one on stage."

"I hope it doesn't give Nic ideas."

"Ideas and actions are two different things," Alison said. "Just think, Deek, a play and my first sex education class, all in one night."

"Hey . . ."

Alison hung up with a mischievous giggle. Let Deek work on that!

At seven o'clock sharp, Nic rang the doorbell.

"Come in, Nic. Alison will be down shortly," Mrs. Grey said.

Right on cue, Alison came down the stairs dressed in a sleeveless lavender dress that brought out the violet lights in her eyes. The dress hugged her slender figure and gave her a cool, sophisticated look.

"You look super," Nic exclaimed. "Beautiful enough to be the goddess Pallas Athena herself. She was gray eyed too, you know."

"Thank you. I guess that settles it, then. I'll have to become a Maiden."

Nic flashed her an engaging smile. "I'm counting on it."

"Enjoy the play," Mrs. Grey said, beaming

fondly at them. "You two certainly make a handsome couple."

Alison winced at her mother's obvious pleasure. Why couldn't she be a little more subtle?

"A dollar for your thoughts."

"What?"

"I said, a dollar for your thoughts," Nic repeated, opening the car door for her. "You were a million miles away."

Alison blushed. "I thought the going rate was a penny."

"Inflation hits everything," Nic said breezily. "Anyway, now that you're back, I was saying I hope you don't mind if Rob and Lucy canceled on us."

"Not at all." Alison replied a shade too quickly to be polite. "Why?"

"Oh, when Rob found out what the play was about he said he'd rather see another Rambo flick."

"He doesn't like Oscar Wilde?"

"Rob never heard of Oscar, I guess. When I asked him if he wanted to see a Wilde play he said sure. He was revved up until I told him some of the plot."

They laughed over Rob's mistake all the way to Rippley. Somehow it made the play even better.

"It was a good production, Nic. I enjoyed it. Thanks for thinking of going," Alison said on their way home.

"Seeing good theater is one of the things I miss," Nic said. "At the academy we went into New York for all the Broadway hits."

"Sexton College brings professional theater groups here," Alison reminded him.

"It's not the same, believe me. But there are other advantages to living in Chandlersville."

"Name five."

"You, for one," Nic replied promptly.

"Thank you. That leaves four."

"Don't rush me, Snowflake."

"How about Carol Hardy, Marilyn Kane, Jenny Byers, and Helen Friedman?" Alison teased, naming a few of the girls Nic had dated in the past year.

"Very good point," Nic said with complete aplomb. "There weren't any girls at the academy. At least, none of the proper sort."

"Proper sort?"

"You know, the kind you can take home to Mother."

"Rather like the play tonight?" Alison asked innocently.

"Proper connections and family? Yes, that's important even today. In fact, that play would work almost as well in a modern setting."

The rest of the way home they discussed how the play could be adapted to modern times. They were still talking when they reached Alison's door.

Nic bent down and kissed her softly. Yet when she pulled away he made no move to stop her.

"It's late," Alison said breathlessly. "I'd better go in."

Nic gave her a lazy smile. "See you at the pool tomorrow?"

"Sure. I have to get in my laps or Miss Stevens will yell at me when school starts."

"See ya then."

" 'Night, Nic. Thanks for a nice evening."

"My pleasure."

Alison closed the door and went upstairs. Everything was so confused. Nic's kiss only made matters worse. She'd liked it. And if she wanted to continue their relationship, she knew she'd have to join the Maidens. Everyone expected her to, anyway. Why was she so hesitant?

Chapter
Two

"What are you doing up so early on a Saturday morning?" Mr. Grey asked as Alison came into the kitchen, fully dressed.

"I have to get in my laps before the pool gets crowded," Alison replied, planting a kiss on his iron-gray hair as she slid into her place at the breakfast table. "What's your excuse?"

"I have a ten o'clock tee time. Golf is more important than sleep—to quote a great philosopher."

"Which great philosopher?" Alison asked, pouring some orange juice and snagging a piece of her father's toast.

"Bob Sproles, my playing partner," Mr. Grey replied. "I know he's a great philosopher because he always says, 'That's life, James,' every time I make a bad shot."

"What does he say when *he* makes a bad shot?"

"That I can't repeat!"

"You'd better eat more than a piece of toast," her mother cautioned, coming into the room. "I can fix eggs or pancakes in a jiffy."

"I never eat much before I swim. Thanks anyway. Dad, will you give me a ride to the club?"

18

"Sure, if you can be ready in, say, ten minutes."

"Can do."

"How was the play?" Mrs. Grey asked.

"Cool. You know, it could be adapted very easily to modern times," Alison answered, washing down the last bite of toast with juice. "Nic and I almost rewrote the whole play on the way home."

Mrs. Grey smiled. "You and Nic have a lot in common, don't you? You should have seen them, James. They made such a handsome couple."

Alison gave her mother an exasperated look. "I wish you'd stop doing that!"

"Doing what?"

"Saying Nic and I make such a handsome couple and all that junk! You sound like a—matchmaker."

"For heaven's sake, Alison," Mrs. Grey said huffily. "I was simply making an observation. Is that forbidden now?"

"Ladies, ladies," Mr. Grey said soothingly, "we don't have time for a full-fledged championship fight this morning. Could we postpone the match until seven this evening? Both contestants will come wearing regulation trunks, white sneakers, and eight-ounce gloves. I will referee. This fight will decide the question . . . What is the question?"

By this time Alison was laughing too hard to answer. The idea of her mother in trunks and boxing gloves was too much! Even Mrs. Grey was smiling.

"All right. If no one can remember the question, then the fight's canceled. Let's go, Alison. I don't want to keep Bob waiting."

"My things are in the hall. Meet you at the car,"

Alison said with another giggle. She really loved her handsome father. She only wished he were around more often to prevent these squabbles.

The pool was deserted except for a few children in the shallow end playing a noisy game of tag. Alison tucked her hair under her cap and did a graceful, flat racing dive into the swim lane.

Water was her element. Cool, blue, and clear, it cradled her. The seemingly effortless rhythm of her strokes calmed her, left her mind free to drift wherever it would. Crawl, four laps; sidestroke, four laps; breaststroke, four laps; repeat; and rest. Refreshed and only a little tired, Alison got out and toweled down.

Deek was waiting for her, her towel spread beside Alison's. "You're looking good! Miss Stevens is going to love you."

"Thanks, but I doubt it. She's never satisfied. Besides, I still haven't cut my hair like she wanted."

"Oh, pooh! It's your swimming that counts. You're going to set some records this year—hair or no hair."

"Um-m-m," Alison said, flopping down on her towel. "I'm so hungry I could eat a goat."

"I don't know about goat, but I could manage a burger and fries. Let's go up to the clubhouse and eat," Deek said. "You can tell me all about your date. Which show was better, on stage or off?"

"On stage," Alison said, and explained about Rob.

Deek laughed so hard Alison was afraid she'd

choke. "What about Nic?" she finally sputtered. "Did you have fun?"

"Yes, we did."

"Well?" Deek said, hopping up. "Go on. Tell all. Let's go eat while you fill in the awesome details. When do you think your mom will call? I swear, this has been the longest morning!"

"Take a chill pill, Deek. If Mom said she'd call, she will. No one holds out under her pressure for long, either."

"You do," Deek replied glumly. "And my mom's a lot like you. Once she makes up her mind, she's hard to change. I'll just die if I have to say no."

"You won't die, Deek. I promise. Mom will talk her into it."

"I hope it's soon. My nervous system's all shot," Deek complained, dancing up the last terrace to the clubhouse. "I'll bet I can't eat a thing."

"Think of the money you'll save. Not to mention the calories."

Deek calmed enough to eat two burgers, a large fries, an apple turnover, and a chocolate milk shake. "So. Are you going to join the Maidens or not?" she asked.

"I haven't had much time to think about it. But I guess I will," Alison replied, pushing away her half-eaten sandwich. Somehow her appetite had vanished.

"Yip-ee-ee!" Deek shouted, causing the other diners to look at her and smile. "Let's go work off some of this lunch."

The pool area was beginning to fill up by the

time they returned. Deek wanted to jump right in, but Alison persuaded her to get wet and sun until their lunch was digested. Both girls flopped on their towels and let the hot sun dry them.

"Mind if I join you?"

Alison looked up and saw Carol Hardy smiling down at her. This was a first. The senior girls, especially the Maidens, usually sat by themselves.

"No, of course not," Deek answered, moving her towel over. "There's plenty of room."

"I hope this weather holds for the house party," Carol said, brushing back the long blond hair that hung straight and sleek to her waist. "I keep threatening to cut this hot mop, but I always chicken out."

"If mine were nice and straight like yours, I'd never cut it," Deek said wistfully.

"If I had your curls, I'd cut mine in a second," Carol declared. "I guess we're never satisfied with what we have."

The girls made small talk and in a very short time were joined by a laughing crowd of boys.

Alison watched with grudging admiration as Carol handled all of them with ease. Carol might be aggressive and determined in other matters, but it sure didn't show around guys. Neither did her brains, although Alison knew she was no dummy. Carol joked and listened to the boys talk about the new football season as if it were the most important thing in the whole world.

"With Nic as our quarterback we're sure to win the Big Eight championship," Butch Miller said.

"That guy can outpass, outrun anybody in the whole district."

"Not without a good line in front of him," declared Carol. Butch was a tackle.

"Carol's right," Deek chimed in. "It takes all eleven guys *plus* a good defense to win."

"Don't forget the subs," Mickey Frazier said. "We're the second line of defense in case you stars get hurt."

"Yeah, Coach says we're only as strong as our bench," Butch agreed.

"Well, we have a strong bench," Carol declared.

"Except for quarterback. We're weak there," Joey reminded them.

"Hey, I'm burning to a crackly crunch," Butch said. "Let's get up a game of polo in the deep end."

"I'll get a ball," volunteered Deek, as they moved toward the water, choosing sides.

"Come join us," Alison said to Tilly Pendergast and Margie Wampler as she passed them, sitting off to one side of the group.

"No, thanks. We were just in," Tilly replied coolly.

Margie said nothing. She turned her head away, but not before Alison saw the tears in her eyes. "Okay," Alison said lamely. "Maybe later."

"You're on my side, Alison," Mickey sang out.

"Not unless I am," Nic said, coming up behind Alison. "We're a team."

The teams were rearranged to accommodate Nic, and they played a noisy, rousing game of polo. Alison enjoyed herself. It wasn't until later, at home, that she remembered Margie's tears.

So Margie and Tilly hadn't been asked to join the Maidens! That surprised Alison. Both girls met all of the qualifications. Why hadn't they been asked? Who were the other six girls? Counting on her fingers, Alison came up with a dozen possibilities. That meant at least six or eight girls would be awfully disappointed. It really wasn't fair. Sighing, she went to answer the phone.

"My folks said yes!" Deek shouted. "Please thank your mom for me."

"I will. Deek, did you know Tilly and Margie didn't get asked?"

"They didn't? Gosh, I would have picked them over me."

"Do you know who the other six are?"

"No. I haven't heard about anyone else. Why?"

"Just curious. It seems a shame to ask only eight girls out of a junior class of five hundred and thirty-seven."

Deek must have sensed Alison was getting cold feet again. "Maybe we can change the rules next year. It's easier to change something from the inside, you know."

"I guess you're right."

"Sure I am. Hey, I almost forgot what else I called for. Want to spend the night with me and go up on the parkway with my folks tomorrow? Dad has a new camera lens he can't wait to try."

"Sure thing!"

"Super! Come on over anytime. Mom's baking chocolate chip cookies to take with us."

"There goes my diet!"

"You can walk it off tomorrow. Hurry on over."

"Be there in a flash. Don't eat all the cookies before I get there."

She didn't get away as soon as she'd thought. First, Nic called and asked her to a movie. He sounded ticked because she had other plans. "Next time you'll have to ask earlier," Alison responded tartly.

"You're absolutely right, Snowflake," Nic said, recovering his good humor. "I'll remember next time. Have a good hike."

"Thanks for the invitation anyway," Alison said contritely. She could have bitten her tongue off for being so sharp.

"Catch you later," Nic said and hung up.

Then, before she could walk away, the phone rang again. Alison answered impatiently.

"Hi, baby sister."

"Hello, old married lady," Alison responded warmly. Ellen was her favorite sister. "What's happening in Richmond?"

"Nothing much. You're the one with the news. Congratulations!"

"When did Mother call you?" Alison asked wearily.

"Five minutes after you received the invitation and fifteen minutes before she called Lisa," Ellen answered, laughing.

"Oh, brother!"

"You know Mother. With her all news travels fast, good and bad. You don't sound exactly overwhelmed, if I may say so. What's wrong?"

"Nothing, Ellen. I was just giving it some serious thought. Mom panicked."

"Now, Alison . . ."

"I know. She only wants what's best for me."

"So do I. But you know more about that than I do. Just because Lisa and I enjoyed something doesn't mean you will. Take your time. Whatever you decide, I'll back you a hundred percent," Ellen said. "In fact, Mother will, too, in the end."

That was what Alison loved about Ellen. She always let Alison decide for herself. "Yeah, I know. Thanks for the support. I'm going to join. Most of my friends are in, so why not?"

"You'll have fun. Honest."

"I did have fun at the pool today. Especially with Nic."

"Mother told me you'd been dating *the* Nic Chandler, emphasis Mother's. Gosh, I remember him as a curly-haired, skinny little kid."

"Well, he still has curly hair, but he's anything but skinny and little. He's an awesome hunk—about six two and a hundred and eighty-five pounds," Alison said, with a note of pride creeping into her voice.

"Stop!" Ellen commanded. "You're making me feel old."

"At twenty-five? Never."

They chatted for a few more minutes before Ellen ended the conversation with an invitation to visit Richmond and shop for her school clothes.

"I'll think about it," Alison promised. "Right now I have to get over to Deek's before she eats all the cookies. Say hi to Frank for me."

"Will do. Give Mom and Dad my love."

* * *

The week before school began wasn't bad. Alison sent in her acceptance on Monday. Lisa, who was a fashion designer for Macy's, called to congratulate her and offered to send her anything she needed from New York. Nic phoned four times, but not for dates because football practice was twice a day now and the guys were pooped. She swam laps every day, except Wednesday when it rained. And she had only one fight with her mother.

The fight was a doozy. What was worse, it was in public.

They had decided against going to Richmond because Alison insisted she didn't need a whole new wardrobe. Then, instead of giving Alison the charge card and letting her go shopping with Deek, Mrs. Grey said, "We'll go together. It will be fun."

Inwardly, Alison groaned. Her taste and her mother's weren't even close. "Sure, it will," she said, resolving to be on her very best behavior.

Her resolve lasted through the first two hours of shopping. It fell apart in the shoe department of Miller and Rhodes.

"You'll need Dock-Sides and knee hose," Mrs. Grey said, seating herself before the shoe salesman. "What size, Alison? A seven or a seven and a half?"

"No," Alison said, still standing.

"A six and a half?" ventured the salesman.

"I don't like Dock-Sides and I hate knee socks," Alison said.

"But you have to have them. They complete your outfit," Mrs. Grey said.

''Why do I have to? I don't like them. They don't look good on me. And I'm not buying any.''

''Really, Alison! All of the Maidens wear them. Especially on Club day,'' Mrs. Grey said slowly, as if explaining to an idiot child.

''Well *I'm* not wearing them!'' Alison said so loudly that several people paused to stare. She turned and walked out of the store. She hated the preppie look. She was willing to go along with the plaid skirt, button-down blouse and sweater, but not those ugly shoes and socks! Yuck!

A few minutes later her mother appeared. ''I've never been so embarrassed in my life!'' she said, slamming the car door.

''I'm sorry. But you might have asked me what I wanted instead of deciding for me.''

''*I* didn't decide. The Maidens have their own dress code. I called Madge Hardy yesterday to find out what you needed, since you didn't seem concerned. Personally, I don't care for those stupid shoes either. But I wanted you to fit in, be like the other girls.''

''A clone. Sixteen little Maidens all in a row. Wonderful!''

Mrs. Grey didn't reply. She drove home in silence, marched into the house, and slammed the door.

Alison stared glumly at the closed door. Sighing, she got out of the car, wandered over to the oak bench. She sat down heavily, drawing her knees up and resting her chin on them.

When had it started, this feeling of a noose tightening around her? Go here. Wear this. Join that.

She hadn't objected before. Everything from nursery school to college had been planned for her. Why was she making a fuss now? The plan had been good enough for Lisa and Ellen. Why not for her? Why couldn't she go along and not make waves? Keep peace in the family?

"Because I don't want to be a clone," she said. "I want to be myself—whoever that is."

Would wearing Dock-Sides and knee socks make her any less of a person? No. And it would make everyone else happy. She was just being selfish and stubborn. Sighing again, she got up, gathered her packages from the car, and went quietly to her room.

Conversation at the dinner table was strained. Mr. Grey did most of the talking. There were long gaps of silence. Alison wanted to say she was sorry but the words stuck in her throat. Finally she gave up and excused herself.

Later her father joined her in the den. Before picking up the evening paper, he said quietly, "Alison, your mother told me what happened this afternoon. I think you were both at fault. Will you please try to get along better with your mother?"

"Yes, sir," Alison said meekly. "I'll try."

"Good," Mr. Grey said and picked up his paper.

Alison fled to her room.

Chapter Three

The candelit room was hushed and solemn.

Eight senior girls clad in short white tunics sat on straight-backed chairs in a semicircle.

The eight junior girls filed in self-consciously, and completed the circle, sitting on the floor. They, too, were dressed in white tunics, the only difference being that their rope sashes were gold, not purple.

Carol Hardy, as Pallas Athena, rose and began the ceremony. "You eight girls have been selected from among many other deserving juniors to become Athena's Maidens. It is an honor. We expect you to prove worthy."

"We welcome you," chorused the seven seniors.

"Our symbols are the olive branch and the owl."

"Hear and remember," intoned the seven.

"Athena and her Maidens are the protectors of the home and civilized life. We honor wisdom and reason. Do you accept our way?"

"We do," the juniors answered raggedly.

"Then hear our history and know which path you must follow," Athena said and sat down.

Marilyn Kane stood up and read the history of Athena's Maidens from a scroll.

Alison shifted to a more comfortable position as Marilyn droned on. She knew the history by heart from Lisa and Ellen. Out of the corner of her eye, she watched the rapt faces of the other juniors. She wanted to punch Deek and make her notice their solemn expressions, but when she turned Deek's face was as immobile as the others. Suppressing a giggle, Alison directed her attention back to the speaker.

"One senior girl is elected to the rank of the goddess Pallas Athena. For one year she guides and nurtures the Maidens. Her word is law. Her wishes, our commands. We are her Maidens."

"We are Pallas Athena's Maidens," chanted the seniors.

"We provide leadership by example," Marilyn continued. "We make our presence known separately and as a group."

"We are sisters."

"Recently, we have acquired brothers. The Sons of Apollo are our brothers. Together we preserve and promote the civilized life of Chandler High, both social and academic," Marilyn said, and sat down.

"Do you wish to join us?" Athena asked, standing before them once more.

"We do."

"Will you keep our secrets, obey our laws, and always be a friend to your sisters and brothers?"

"We will."

"Rise and be pinned by your sisters with our

symbol of wisdom. You will wear this owl at all times to remind you and others of who you are—Maidens of Athena.''

The new members rose and were pinned by their sisters. Pallas Athena pinned Alison. Lights were turned on and the candles blown out. The room filled with excited, happy chatter.

"Thank heavens that's over," Alison whispered to Deek. "One more round of that Greek chorus and I'd have barfed!''

"They were pretty awful, weren't they?" Deek said, giggling.

"Awful isn't the word I had in mind."

"Sh-h! Someone might hear you."

"Might hear what?" asked Carol, gliding up behind them.

"Might hear Alison say she was thirsty and think she was rude," Deek answered quickly.

"That can be remedied," Carol said. "Hey, everyone. Refreshments are on the deck, courtesy of Mr. and Mrs. Kane."

As everyone rushed from the room, Carol pulled Alison aside. "Just a moment, Alison. I want to talk to you."

"Sure," Alison said, blushing. Carol wasn't buying Deek's story for one minute.

"Good. I just wanted to tell you that you've been selected as my Handmaiden. That means, among other things, that you'll be groomed to take my place next year."

Alison was stunned. Why her, of all people? Carol was watching her with an amused glint in her eyes. "Well—uh—thanks. I'll do my best."

"I'm sure you will," Carol said, linking her arm through Alison's. "Let's join the others. I could use a drink myself."

The evening turned into a giant slumber party. The girls talked and giggled all night in spite of the fact they had to be up early Saturday to prepare for the onslaught of eighteen hungry, fun-loving guys.

Saturday dawned clear and promising, a perfect day for one last joyous burst of freedom before nine long months of school. The guys arrived at ten o'clock, bringing more food and drink to an already overstocked house.

The cabin, the grounds, and the beach rang with laughter and music. Alison played softball and volleyball, pitched horseshoes, and swam to her heart's content. Nic was always, flatteringly, beside her.

After the evening cookout, Alison went upstairs to freshen up and bumped into Deek coming out of the bathroom.

"Oops! Sorry about that," Deek said, peeking behind Alison. "What? No Nic? How did you manage that?"

"It wasn't easy."

"See? I told you it would be fun. I'm in heaven. Have you noticed Ken Ritchie? He's a real hunk! He never paid any attention to me before and my locker's only two away from his."

"Maybe he got contact lenses this summer."

"Whatever! He's paying attention now," Deek replied, dancing away.

Alison shook her head. What could Deek possibly see in Ken? He was a hunk, all right. Two hundred and twenty-five pounds of beefy tackle and dumb as a brick. What did they find to talk about?

When she came downstairs she found Nic and Rob on the deck in a deep discussion. Rob saw her and broke away. "Having fun, Alison? Great party, huh?"

"Terrific."

Nic took her elbow. "We're headed to the beach. Arnie has his stereo system all wired and ready to go. See ya later, Rob."

"Don't do anything I wouldn't do," Rob said, leering at Alison. "Remember what I told you, Nic."

"Jerk," Nic muttered under his breath. He took Alison's hand, and they strolled to the beach and joined the dancing crowd.

After an hour or so, Nic said, "I don't know about you, but this music is beginning to make my ears ring. Let's take advantage of that moon and grab some peace and quiet. Want to canoe over to Crescent Island?"

Alison was hot and pleasantly tired. Crescent Island looked cool and inviting, floating in the middle of Shandy Lake. "Sure, let's go."

Quietly they slipped away to the boat dock. Nic found the paddles, and they shoved off in the small silver canoe, hugging the shoreline until they were out of sight of the beach party.

A full moon hung in the sky, lighting their way with a magical glow. Echoes of the party music rolled over the water and Nic hummed along as he paddled.

Alison didn't speak. She just enjoyed the ride,

the moon, and the gentle splash of water as the paddle dipped in and out of the water.

Nic beached the canoe quietly against the grassy bank.

Alison jumped out and swung the canoe around for Nic. Laughing, because he got his sneakers wet anyway, they pulled the canoe up on the grass, and Nic spread out the blanket he brought.

For a few minutes Alison sat with Nic's arm around her, enjoying the beauty of the moonlit lake. Then, very gently, Nic pushed her back on the blanket and kissed her.

It was a sweet kiss. Like the first taste of a chocolate bar, Alison thought, you can hardly wait for more.

Nic didn't make her wait long. The next kiss was longer and better. Alison responded with enthusiasm and lost count. Only when she felt herself losing control did she sit up and push Nic away. "I think we'd better cool it, Nic," she said huskily.

"Not this time, Snowflake," he said, pulling her down beside him.

Alison was too surprised to resist when Nic pinned her down with his arms. She could see his blue eyes glittering only inches above her face. A kaleidoscope of thoughts cascaded through her head. "Why do you call me Snowflake?" was what she blurted out.

Nic's mouth curled in a smile that didn't reach his eyes. "Because that's what you are. Cold and as hard to catch as a snowflake. An ice maiden. Look but don't touch."

But he was touching! Kissing her neck, her

cheek, her eyes, and her lips, hard. Alison broke the kiss by tossing her head, and struggled to sit up. "Nic, don't be silly. Why are you acting like this? Who says I'm an ice maiden?"

"Everyone," Nic replied. "All the guys you won't make out with, won't even date twice. But Nic's going to thaw the ice maiden tonight. Yes, sir!"

Alison struggled harder. But the more she fought the more Nic seemed to enjoy it. "Come on, baby, fight! Makes the prize that much sweeter."

"Nic, let me up! Let's go back to the party."

"We'll go back," he said, "but not until I've won my hundred-dollar bet."

His words shocked Alison into immobility.

"That's better. Kick back and enjoy," Nic said smugly.

Just as she did before a big race, Alison made her body relax. "Okay. It's not a fate worse than death, especially with you."

"Why, thank you, ma'am."

"One thing," she continued, trying to sound anything but angry. "Who's the bet with? I ought to know who's paying for my services."

Nic hooted with laughter. "You're okay. Really cool. I can't tell you exactly who. Let's just say this whole deal's a setup."

"You mean our dates, the Maidens, and everything?"

"You got it, Snowflake. This is part of your initiation, O Handmaiden of Athena." He silenced her with his mouth.

Handma—? Carol! A sick, betrayed feeling swept over Alison. Why? Why would Carol do this?

Nic mistook her confusion for compliance and relaxed his grip. Alison brought her knee up with all the force she could muster.

Nic howled in pain and rolled into a ball.

In one fluid motion, Alison was on her feet, racing for the water. She barely waited to come out of her shallow dive before she began stroking for shore.

Nic was on his knees, shouting for her to come back.

Alison paid no heed. Red-hot anger and humiliation flowed through her. She swam harder than she ever had before, the much-practiced rhythm taking over and leaving her mind a jumble.

One hundred dollars . . . a setup . . . all those dates . . . a phony . . . Athena's Maidens . . . Carol Hardy, pimp . . . rotten, deceitful Nic . . . The canoe! Would he come after her? Swim faster. . . . No! Don't break rhythm. . . . Don't panic. . . .

Chest heaving, Alison felt her foot strike shore. Barely pausing to catch her breath, she began to run. Anger drove her forward. Caution made her avoid the people by the campfire. Once she reached the cabin, she ran upstairs and flung her things into the suitcase. She didn't even stop long enough to change out of her dripping clothes.

"Hey, what's wrong? Where are you going?" Carol stood in the doorway with a look of concern on her face.

Rage almost choked Alison. "Get out of my

way," she said icily. "I'm leaving you creeps. I wouldn't be a part of this crowd if you were the last people on earth."

Carol stepped aside. "What's the matter with you? Are you sick or something?"

"I'm not the one who's sick. Go find Nic and collect your money," Alison said, running down the stairs.

"What money? Is Nic sick? Where is he?"

"On Crescent Island, nursing his wounded pride and his crotch," Alison snarled as she raced out the door.

She drove home through a curtain of tears. She felt betrayed, by her so-called friends, by Nic, by her own body. How could she have responded to such a crud? Why hadn't she followed her first instincts? Gone her own way? Oh, no. She'd taken the easy way out. Pleased everyone but herself. And look where it landed her.

The house was dark when she coasted into the driveway. Shivering in her damp clothes, Alison quietly let herself in and tiptoed upstairs. She couldn't face sympathy or questions now.

Once in the safety of her own room, she stripped off her damp clothes, pulled out a flannel gown, and crept into bed. It was hours before she could stop shaking and go to sleep.

Chapter
Four

"Alison, are you all right?" Mrs. Grey called, opening the door and peering inside.

Alison rolled over and sat up, staring groggily at her mother. Last night's episode came back in a sickening rush. "I—I'm fine, Mother."

"Well, you don't look fine. You're as white as your sheets. Did you get ill at the party? Why didn't you wake us?"

"I didn't get ill. I got mad! I've dropped out of the Maidens and I'm not going back. No matter what you or anyone else says!"

Mrs. Grey looked stunned, but managed to say in her usual cool voice, "That's your decision. Why don't you shower, and I'll fix you a nice breakfast before church."

"No, thanks. I'm not hungry. And I don't want to go to church." Without another word she tossed the cover aside and marched into her bathroom. She shut the door firmly behind her.

Alison stayed in her room until her parents left. Then she went downstairs and ate some toast. It sat uneasily in her stomach. Nic, Carol, and Crescent Island played over and over in her head.

After church, Mrs. Grey came upstairs and knocked on Alison's door again.

"Come in," Alison called wearily. She knew she'd have to tell her mother something. But what?

"Well, it's a good thing you did come home, for whatever reason," Mrs. Grey said. "The police had to break up a fight at the Kanes' cabin last night. Rob Warren was taken to the hospital with a badly broken nose."

A vengeful wave washed over Alison. She wished it could have been Nic!

"Do you have any idea what it was about?" her mother asked, watching Alison's face carefully.

"Rob and Nic compete in everything. It was probably something trivial."

"Boys will be boys, I suppose. I'm just glad you weren't involved. Why *did* you come home if you weren't ill?"

"I had a major disagreement with Nic and Carol," Alison replied, deciding on truth—or partial truth. "It seems reasonable to me, if you don't like the leaders you shouldn't be in the club. I don't like either one." Her tone said, "This is final. End of discussion."

Her mother sighed and shook her head. "Are you coming down for lunch?"

"I just had breakfast. I'll wait for dinner."

"All right. Suit yourself."

"I won't starve, Mother. I plan to read and get my clothes ready for school. Those activities won't burn many calories."

Without replying, Mrs. Grey walked out.

Deek called at one o'clock. "Tell her I'm busy," Alison called downstairs. "I'm washing my hair."

Mrs. Grey relayed the message, but Deek was not to be denied. An hour later she was at Alison's door. "Knock, knock," she said brightly. A little too brightly, Alison thought. "Your mom said to come on up. Did you finish your hair? It looks great, as usual. So give! Why'd you leave? You missed all the excitement."

"Mother told me about the brawl."

"Boy, you should have seen it! Mr. Kane was as drunk as a skunk, but he tried to stop it. Got a black eye for his trouble. It would have been funny if Nic and Rob hadn't been trying to kill each other."

"Too bad they didn't succeed."

"Hey, what's eating you? Even before all this happened, Carol said you quit the Maidens and left in a huff. How come?"

"Ask Miss Hardy. She knows," Alison snarled.

"No, she doesn't. She asked me to come over and find out."

"Oh, now you're her lackey?"

Deek looked bewildered and a little angry. "I'm not anybody's lackey. I'm your friend, remember?"

Alison saw Deek's hurt expression and felt ashamed. "I'm sorry, Deek. I didn't mean to take my mad out on you. We're friends. No matter what happens."

"Good," Deek said, her eyes filling with tears. "Because I may have to resign, too, if my parents hear about the police and all."

"Don't worry, Deek. I'll bet the Chandlers will have everything swept under a convenient rug by now. Can't let the all-American hero have a police record, can we?"

"I guess you're right," Deek said, brightening a little. "Nic's dad came out to the cabin immediately. He talked to the police before he dragged Nic away. The Warrens didn't file charges."

"See? Damage control. Nobody will talk about it either, if Mr. All-Powerful Chandler says keep quiet."

"Mr. Chandler was pretty steamed. I heard him tell Nic he was sending him back to the academy on the first plane. Do you think he meant it?"

"I certainly hope so!"

"Oh, Alison, you don't mean that! What about our football team? We don't have anyone half as good as Nic. We open Friday with Oak Hall."

"I don't care if we lose every game! If it means getting rid of Nic Chandler, I'm all for it!"

"That must have been some fight. Want to clue me in?"

"No." Alison's glare warned Deek to shut up.

"Okay. Uh—you doin' anything for Labor Day?"

"No."

"Ken's taking me to the last day of the county fair. See you at school Tuesday bright and early?"

"Sure."

Alison sat in her window seat and watched Deek pedal down the drive. Should she have told Deek? The mere thought made her stomach churn. Why tell? What good would it have done? Nothing had happened, except to her pride. The memory was humiliating enough without sharing it. Was she being fair? What if Carol tried the pimping trick on Deek? No, this was strictly Nic's little scheme, aided by Carol. If Nic really was gone, there would be no danger. Besides, Deek wanted to be one of Athena's Maidens. Why ruin it for her? All that sister stuff was fine for some people. It suited Lisa and Ellen and lots of others, but not her. Giving in to others' wishes was her first mistake.

No! Joining the Maidens was her *second* mistake. The first mistake was being taken in by Nic. She'd swallowed his bait, hook, line, and sinker. She knew his reputation and went out with him anyway. He'd been a perfect gentleman, a smooth talker, and a fun date. She'd been dazzled by his flattering attention. Even liked his kisses. Be honest! More than liked, been turned on. Just not ready to go all the way. If Nic had been more patient, not told her about the bet . . .

A wave of self-disgust swept over her. It won't happen again, she vowed. Never, *ever* will I be taken in by a handsome face and a smooth line. I have learned my lesson.

Chapter
Five

Tuesday, September 5. Her first day as a junior. Alison dressed carefully. Usually she looked forward to the first day of school. Today she was antsy. She'd rejected the most popular, most powerful group in school. How would people react to that? More important, how was she going to act when she ran into Nic and Carol? Giving her hair a final stroke, she went down to breakfast.

"My, you look pretty this morning," her father said. "Are you sure you're going to school?"

Alison grinned at him. He always had a way of making her feel good. "Have to impress those little freshmen, you know. We upperclassmen have an image to uphold."

"You're upholding your end," Mr. Grey assured her. "Want a ride?"

"No, thanks. I'm early. I think I'll walk."

"Perhaps the fresh air will clear your head, and you'll change your mind about becoming a recluse," Mrs. Grey said, teasing her.

"I'm not a recluse. I'm just not a Maiden!"

"I call staying in your room for two days reclusive behavior."

"Ladies, ladies! Let's not begin another war of words," Mr. Grey said soothingly.

"Right. I'm out of here," Alison said, picking up her backpack.

Chandler High was a sprawling, modern complex that resembled a junior college more than a high school. Students spilled out of every doorway onto the walks and lawn. The noise, laughter, and general confusion of the first day of school were familiar and reassuring as Alison made her way to the office to pick up her schedule.

Deek was waiting for her at her old locker. "Did you hear? It's true! Mr. Chandler sent Nic away. We don't have a quarterback!"

"Oh, bummer! How will we manage without Mr. Wonderful? So how's your schedule?"

"Lousy. I have Hooper for chemistry. How's yours?"

"Not too shabby," Alison said, twirling her combination. The door stuck as it always did. She gave it a swift kick and it popped open.

"I thought for sure you'd change lockers this year," Deek said, giggling.

"Why? I'm used to the idiosyncrasies of this one. It likes to be kicked." Alison put up her notebooks, and pulled out her blue card to check the number of her homeroom.

"Hey, you got in advanced life sciences with Dr. Dorn," Deek said, peering over her shoulder. "Why you want to take that class, I don't know. Everyone says she assigns so much work you never get to do anything else."

"She's a good teacher, even if she is hard," Alison said loyally. "I had her last year in biology, remember? I like Dr. Dorn."

"We don't have any classes together," wailed Deek. "You don't have a study hall!"

"A.L.S throws everything off," Alison explained. "I have to have a two-hour block of time. One for lecture, one for lab. That's why mostly seniors take it."

"Seniors and junior brains," Deek said affectionately. "Well, to each his own brand of poison. I'll have my hands full with this load. Whose homeroom are you in?"

"Spangler's."

"I'm next door in Hopkins's. I guess that's as close as we'll get all day," Deek said as they strolled down the hall.

They joined a group that had collected outside the doors of 113 and 115. A second of embarrassed silence followed. No one looked directly at Alison.

"Hi," Tilly Pendergast finally said. The rest chimed in.

Mrs. Hopkins opened her door and half of the students filed inside.

"See you later," Deek called.

Alison nodded, her cheeks burning. She knew very well that she'd been the topic of conversation. A few minutes later Mr. Spangler opened his door, and she slipped gratefully inside.

The rest of the day went the same way. No one made any effort to talk to her. Actually, it felt as if everyone was avoiding her, especially some of her old friends like Tilly and Margie. At least, Alison thought, I haven't run into Carol. Be happy with small blessings.

When the last bell rang she breathed a sigh of relief. Surely things would be better tomorrow. She hurried to her locker, dragged out her gym bag, and went to the pool.

The familiar smells of chlorine and damp tile were welcome. No one else had hurried down to begin practice under Miss Stevens's critical eye, thank goodness. She changed quickly into her green practice suit, tucked her hair into her cap, and went into the empty pool area.

The Olympic pool was an impressive L-shaped complex. Much better than other pools in the region. The blue water beckoned. Alison dived in and fell into the steady, familiar beat of her crawl as she lapped the pool. The rhythm soothed her, washed away the tension of the day. Here in her element of blue calm she could forget, concentrate only on her turns and her breathing.

A shrill whistle broke her rhythm. Alison looked up and saw a room full of people. Two girls were even in the pool with her!

"Out of the water, girls. I want to talk to you a moment before we begin practice," Miss Stevens said.

Alison and the other two climbed out quickly.

"You're looking good, Alison," Miss Stevens said. "Tuck a little more on your turns."

"Yes, ma'am," Alison replied, smiling. A good word from Miss Stevens was to be treasured.

"The practice schedule for this six weeks will be

one hour after school, Monday through Wednesday, and two hours on Saturday morning.''

The team groaned.

Miss Stevens ignored it, and continued. ''If you feel you can't meet this schedule, please drop out now. Believe me, you'll be glad when we get into competition. We are a young team. We lost six varsity members by graduation, and have only one senior. However, with hard work we can do well. The varsity team will be chosen at the end of the six weeks. So swim hard, girls! And remember, no one makes the team with even one failing grade— that includes D's. So keep those grades up, or all your work and mine will be wasted. Okay, hit the water!''

Practice went well. When the all-clear whistle blew, Alison was pleasantly tired and relaxed. On the way to the locker room she bumped into Nancy Miller, the one senior on the team who also happened to be one of Athena's Maidens.

Before Alison could apologize, Nancy snapped, ''Watch where you're going, Miss High and Mighty.''

Alison's tension was back full force. ''It was an accident, Nancy.''

Nancy glared at her and proceeded to gather a crowd around her, telling a joke. Alison was pointedly excluded.

Hurt, but refusing to let the others see it, Alison dressed, gathered her things, and strolled out with her head held high.

I don't care, she told herself as she walked home. Who needs them? They aren't going to keep me from swimming with their silly snubs. I'm going to make the varsity team whether they talk to me or not!

The following days brought more of the same treatment. Nothing was ever said out in the open, only more silences when she joined groups. Old friends passed her in the halls and looked the other way.

Alison's reaction was to ignore them. She looked straight ahead and pretended she didn't see them either. Her manner was such that *twice* freshmen mistook her for a teacher. One asked her to sign his hall pass, and the other wanted help with her class schedule.

Friday night's football game was a near disaster. Chandler defeated Oak Hall 7–6. Chandler was supposed to crush them on their way to a district, and maybe a state, championship.

On Monday, people were still grumbling about their team's poor showing. Alison was standing in the lunch line and couldn't help overhearing the conversation of the guys in front of her.

"If Nic had been here the score would have been fifty-seven to zero!"

"Man, that Clayton is the pits! What dude fumbles the snap from center four times and has the nerve to say he's a quarterback?"

"Cut him some slack. He only had a week to practice."

"Get real, man. We might as well kiss that championship goodbye."

Alison felt a twinge of regret. Everyone had counted on this being Chandler's year. Facing Nic would have been unpleasant, but there was no reason for the whole school to suffer. Not for the first time, she wondered why Mr. Chandler had yanked Nic out. One fight wasn't much of an excuse. Guys fought all the time. She didn't think it was because of that stupid bet, either. Nic was too macho to tell anyone about that.

"This seat's taken," Rob Warren growled as she started to sit down at a partially filled table. "Sit somewhere you're welcome."

Her face a fiery red, Alison moved to another table. No one looked at her. No one joined her.

After that she was very careful where she sat at lunch. And she brought a book along every day. That way no one bothered her or had to talk to her. Still, she felt the totality of the snubs she was getting was more than she deserved.

By accident Alison found out why the rest of her classmates felt so strongly. She was eating her solitary lunch one day when Dr. Dorn stopped by her table. "Alison, would you do me a favor?"

"Sure."

"I have an appointment in my office at one, so I'm going to be a few minutes late to class. Would you take these keys and unlock the supply room? Put slide boxes thirty-three through forty-two out. The students can be set up when I get there."

"I'm finished here. I'll go right now."

"Thanks."

Alison put up her tray and went to the science wing. She was in the supply room getting down the slides when she heard voices in the classroom.

"A broad? A girl in this school?"

"That's what I heard."

"Can you beat that? We lose the best quarter-back we ever had because of a dumb broad!"

"Who told you?" chimed in a third voice.

"I heard it from someone who was there."

"I heard it was because of the fight. Nic busted Rob's nose but good."

"Nah. Nic knocked up some girl and his old man yanked him out of harm's way."

"What girl?"

"Use your head. Who was Nic dating?"

"Alison Grey?"

"Bingo!"

"For sure?"

"I kid you not. I wish Nic had kept his pants zipped and his hands in his pockets. If he'd saved his stuff for the football field we'd be four and oh, not two and two."

There was more but Alison didn't hear it. She clapped her hands over her ears, looking desperately for another way out besides going into the classroom. The supply room was shared by two labs. If only Dr. Dorn's key would fit the other door . . .

It fit. Shaking with relief, Alison escaped through the empty classroom to the restroom. Five minutes later, looking composed, she walked into A.L.S. and announced, "Dr. Dorn will be late. We're to get out microscopes and set them up." It was the hardest thing she'd ever had to do.

How do you fight a rumor like that? You can't stand up in assembly and deny it. And you can't ignore it. Not in your mind. Alison felt as if everyone was looking at her abdomen. Or waiting for her to be absent from school for a few days. There was nothing to do but be in school *every* day, looking healthy and slender.

Each successive Monday was worse. Chandler lost two games in a row before beating Longwood 14–7. Then it was Homecoming Week. The school buzzed with excitement. Every available space was covered with banners and posters.

For the first time, Alison wasn't nominated for Homecoming Queen, which didn't surprise her. It did hurt when she wasn't nominated for student council. She pretended she didn't care. She let the activity swirl around her and kept her distance. She kept up her usual routine—classes, swimming, trips to the library, and an occasional visit from Deek. Somehow she survived.

But the strain of keeping up appearances and holding everything inside was taking its toll. Alison found she was unable to concentrate. Facts slipped through her mind like water through a sieve.

Alison knew her mother was concerned about her and wasn't surprised by the late-night phone call.

"Hi. What's new, little sis?" Ellen said brightly.

"Hi, Ellen. Nothing's new. I'm fine. Mom and Dad are fine."

"That's not what Mother said."

"Oh, boy! She's called up the reserves."

"She's worried about you. She says you've become a hermit. A silent recluse. What gives?"

"Her social status is threatened because I didn't join the Maidens."

"That's not fair, Alison, and you know it!"

"Okay. I'm sorry. I'm going through a rough patch, Ellen. Nothing major. I'll handle it."

Ellen was ticked. "That's your typical response, Alison. You always were the odd one out! Lisa and I ran to Mother with every bruise or problem. Talked her ears off. Silly woman thought that's what daughters did. Then along comes Alison."

Alison felt her face flush. "I'm just different, Ellen."

"I know. The question is, Are you smart enough to ask for help if you need it?"

"Yes," Alison answered with as much conviction as she could muster.

"Okay. But if you need a totally biased, in-your-favor person to talk to, you know my number."

"Thanks, El."

"Better expect a phone call from Lisa, too."

"Gosh, Mother really is in a tizzy!"

"Make nice, little sister, or I'll come home and give you a knuckle rub."

"Do my best. Bye, Ellen."

Lisa's call followed much the same line, but this time Alison was prepared and was able to reassure her without too much hassle. Fending off her sisters was much easier than fending off Deek. As persistent as a pesky mosquito, Deek continued to ask questions. She also tried in every way possible to draw Alison into the high school scene.

"Let's call it quits," Deek said one night when Alison was helping her with algebra. "Let's go to Lucky's for a Coke. I'm parched."

"No! I don't want to. We have Cokes in the fridge."

"Come on, Alison. It will do us good to get out for a while and be with the gang."

"I don't have a gang anymore. I don't need one."

"Oh, pooh! Everyone needs friends. You're becoming a hermit."

"I am not!" Alison blazed. "And for gosh sakes, Deek, do me a favor. Stop saying, 'Oh, pooh!' That went out with hoop skirts and high-button shoes."

Deek jumped off the bed and glared at Alison. "Get off my case, Alison. I don't need hassling from you! Mom hassles me about my grades. Dad hassles me about spending too much money. Coach Brown hassles me about spending too much time with basketball. Coach Harmon hassles me about spending too much time cheerleading. The Maidens hassle me because I can't drive a car. From you, I don't need any grief over how I talk!"

Alison knew Deek was too kind to mention the hassle she was getting about her. "I'm sorry, Deek. I really am. My moods have been pretty foul lately. I didn't mean to take it out on you."

Deek sat down on the bed again. "Why don't you tell me what's going on, Alison?"

Alison's protective shield immediately dropped in place. She wanted to tell Deek, but the words wouldn't come out. The humiliation was still too great. "Let's make a deal, Deek. I won't hassle you, if you won't hassle me. Okay?"

"Okay," Deek agreed with a sigh. "I think you're being pig-headed but I'll play along."

"It's like a skinned knee," Alison explained. "The sore heals faster if you don't pick at the scab."

"Yeah," Deek said, "but I never could resist picking. I've got scars to prove it."

"I know," Alison said, laughing. "Remember when you had chicken pox, and your mom made you wear mittens?"

"And you came over and scratched my back! Mom was furious with you."

That escapade brought back more memories. They talked for hours, and Alison was in a much better mood when Deek went home. Maybe the worst is over, she thought as she prepared for bed.

She was wrong.

Chapter
Six

"Alison, will you stop by my office this afternoon after school?" Dr. Dorn asked as Alison walked out of advanced life sciences class Monday afternoon.

"Yes, ma'am," Alison replied. A request to go to Dr. Dorn's office was a command. Dr. Dorn was Chandler's assistant principal as well as a teacher.

At three-fifteen, Alison rapped lightly on Dr. Dorn's door.

"Come in, Alison," Dr. Dorn invited. "Have a seat. We need to have a little talk."

Dr. Frances Dorn was an attractive, auburn-haired woman in her late thirties. A petite person with a great passion for teaching, she had a reputation for being hard, fair, and caring.

Alison sat in one of the comfortable leather chairs. She was puzzled. What was this all about? She searched Dr. Dorn's face for a clue.

Dr. Dorn looked serious. "Alison, you were one of the few juniors allowed to take A.L.S. You were chosen because of your aptitude for science and your past grades. I feel that was a mistake. We are approaching the end of the first six weeks, and you have a high D or a low C, depending on your exam grade. The course gets more difficult. I'm very sorry, but I believe it would be better for you if you withdrew with an incomplete."

Alison was in shock. "Withdrew?"

"Yes. I know you're a swimmer trying out for the varsity team. Miss Stevens is counting on you. Failing A.L.S. would make you ineligible. Just because I made a mistake there's no need for you or the swim team to suffer."

The words stung Alison like a slap in the face. "I've never made a D in my life! I didn't realize I was doing so badly. You didn't make a mistake. I can do the work."

"I thought so. But you aren't doing it. You started out well, but your last few papers have been terrible. You've stopped participating in class and your lab work is sloppy. I thought you'd snap out of this slump, but you haven't."

"I can't. I don't know how," Alison said in desperation. "I can't concentrate. Everything slips right through my head."

"You have seemed preoccupied. Do you want to tell me what's bothering you?"

"No," Alison said, lifting her chin. "I can handle it myself." It was bad enough to have her favorite teacher think she was a dummy.

"Does it have anything to do with Athena's Maidens and Nic Chandler?"

Surprised, Alison nodded.

"I thought that might be it," Dr. Dorn said with a sigh. "Alison, it might surprise you to know that I have been trying to get rid of the Maidens for a

long time. They are not a school-sponsored club.
They wield entirely too much power and cause too
much pain. They've been quasi-sanctioned by the
school administration for far too long. They aren't
good for the students or the school. Teachers don't
live in a vacuum. I know about your refusal to join
this exclusive clique. What I don't understand is
why you've closed yourself off from everyone
else.''

"Because everyone hates me,'' Alison blurted.

"Why should everyone hate you?''

"The Maidens hate me because I was the first
girl *ever* to turn them down. Everyone else hates
me because we don't have Nic Chandler for quarterback. We were supposed to win the district and
maybe the state titles this year.''

"Oh, for goodness' sakes, Alison, no one knows
whether we could have done that or not! Even if
Nic had been here, it wouldn't have been a cer-
tainty. What it is is a good excuse for losing. In
any event, Nic's departure wasn't your fault.''

Alison blushed but remained silent.

Dr. Dorn stared at her for a long moment. "All
right, Alison, I'm going to break one of my hard
and fast rules: Never talk about one student to another. But you are worth saving. Nic Chandler was
here on probation. His father's, not ours. Leland
Chandler sat in that chair and told me of his bargain
with Nic. Nic wanted to come back to public
school. He was tired of private schools and their
restrictions. Mr. Chandler agreed Nic could finish
high school here *if* he promised to stay out of trou-

ble. One infraction of the rules and back he went to the academy.

"Nic has been a constant headache for the Chandlers. He's handsome and intelligent, but he has a wild streak that no one has been able to control. That's why he was sent to private schools in the first place. Well, Nic's good behavior lasted almost a year. The fight with Rob broke the bargain, as far as Mr. Chandler was concerned. He sent Nic back to the academy the very next day. So why should people blame you? Nic knew the consequences of his actions."

Dr. Dorn's information explained Mr. Chandler's action but it didn't solve her problem. "You know why Nic left, but other people don't. They make up reasons. Most of them include me. Some things they are saying aren't very nice. They treat me like a—a Typhoid Mary."

"And exactly how is that?"

"They snub me, avoid me, spread nasty rumors about me."

"And your reaction to all of these rumors has been to withdraw. Miss Stevens tells me you have had absolutely nothing to do with any other team member. I see you eat alone. Come to class alone. You are doing what those few people want. You're punishing yourself."

"People don't even talk to me."

"Maybe you haven't given them a fair chance. I admire poise, but sometimes your aloof attitude is more like a prickly porcupine. It warns people off," Dr. Dorn said, smiling to take the sting out of her words.

"I'll think about what you've said," Alison replied. She knew Dr. Dorn had made a fair assessment, but her words still hurt.

"I hope you will, because it's affecting your schoolwork. I think my suggestion is a good one. Take an incomplete in A.L.S., and give yourself some time."

Alison sat still, lost in thought for a few seconds. "Can I take the six-weeks exam before I give up?"

"If you take the exam, I can't give you an incomplete. If you fail, you'll be off the swim team. The exam's next Friday. That doesn't give you much time, Alison."

"I know. Maybe I absorbed some of the material by osmosis. Anyway, I'd like to give it a shot. Please?"

A smile of encouragement flicked over Dr. Dorn's face. "All right. You'd better scoot home and start your review. The exam won't be easy."

"Yours never are," Alison replied, smiling. "Thanks—for everything."

"You're welcome. Good luck."

I'll need it, Alison thought grimly, as she ran home. I'll need all the luck I can beg, borrow, or steal.

Chapter
Seven

Alison studied every spare minute during the day and into the wee hours of every night. She read until the words in the book blurred and ran together in a river of black type. Then she would close the book and review in her head. It pleased her that this time the material stuck.

Mrs. Grey made no objections to the late hours and skimpy meals. She seemed happy to have Alison caring about something again. Late Thursday evening, she knocked softly on Alison's door.

"Come in," Alison called impatiently.

"I thought you might like some hot chocolate and cookies," she said, tentatively holding out a tray.

"Thanks, Mother. I could use a break."

"How's it going?"

"Pretty good, I think. I didn't realize we'd covered so much material. I don't seem to remember much. I must have been a space case."

"Welcome back," Mrs. Grey said, giving Alison's dark hair an encouraging pat as she turned to leave.

On impulse, Alison grabbed her hand and gave it a squeeze. "I'm sorry I've been such a pain."

"You haven't been a pain, Alison. We've just been concerned. We didn't know how to help since we didn't know what was wrong."

"I know. I had to work it out for myself. I haven't yet, but I'm on my way."

"Good," Mrs. Grey said with a smile. "You know, I've even missed our fights."

"You did? Well, let's see, maybe we can go shopping—"

"On second thought, I didn't miss them *that* much!"

"I'll think of something else," Alison promised.

"I'm sure you will," her mother said with a wink as she closed the door.

Alison drank the hot chocolate and nibbled the cookies as she read the last two chapters for the *third* time. She felt much less tense after her talk with her mother. For a change, she felt as if she could sleep. She'd done all she could. Tomorrow would decide if it was enough.

The written exam took a little over an hour. The practicum took a little less than an hour. When she finished, Alison was exhausted but pleased. She hadn't drawn any total blanks.

Deek was waiting at her locker. "There you are. Hey, you look as beat as I feel. I thought I was going to miss you. The cheerleading van leaves for Granby in five minutes. How'd it go?"

"Pretty good. With Dr. Dorn's tests you're never sure."

"I've called you a couple of times this week, but your mom said you were studying," Deek said, a note of disbelief in her voice.

"I had to cram. I was about to fail A.L.S. How'd your exams go?"

"You? Failing? Get real, Alison."

"I had a very low C or a high D. That's failing for a place on the swim team, Deek."

"Well, join the unhappy crowd! Algebra II is killing me. I'll be lucky to pull a C. With the Maidens, cheerleading, and basketball, I haven't had much time to hit the books."

Alison grinned. "Yeah, school subjects have a way of messing up our carefree high school days."

"Yeah. I think it's a plot by adults. If I see one more book I'll barf."

"Hey, Deek! Come on. We're waiting on you," John Felton, the head cheerleader, yelled.

"I'm coming!" Deek shouted. "I'd better go before he has a nervous breakdown. Call me?"

"Sure. I plan to sleep all day tomorrow, but I'll call you Sunday. I hope we win this game."

"Me, too," Deek said, and ran down the hall, ignoring glares from two teachers.

Chandler High did win. The only long faces Monday morning were on students who did not do well on their exams. The grades were posted outside of each teacher's door.

Alison joined the gaggle gathered outside of the science labs. A lump sat in the middle of her throat and refused to go down. Amid groans and satisfied smiles, Alison pushed her way forward until she could see the A.L.S. sheets. Her name was third from the top: Grey, Alison: class exam, 94; lab, 97; six weeks, *B*. The lump in her throat became a wide grin.

A quick trip to the phys. ed. department brought another smile. She was officially a member of the varsity swim team! Her happiness lasted through her other classes, although she hadn't done as well on the other exams. She managed to pull a B average.

This time in A.L.S. she paid attention and took complete notes.

At the end of the lecture period, Dr. Dorn said, "Since we are beginning a new area, bacteriology, you will have new lab partners. I intend to change your partners every six weeks. By changing, you will learn to match skills and improve your own techniques. So as I call out your names, please take your books to the appropriate lab table."

Dana Wilson, Alison's partner, gave her a faint smile as she gathered her things.

Alison flushed. I'll bet she's glad to be rid of me. I wasn't much help the last six weeks.

"Table four, Grey and Mendoza."

Alison moved across the room and sat beside a stranger. To be honest, she hadn't paid much attention to who was in her class. They were mostly seniors. Though his face looked familiar, she didn't know his name. "Hi," she said, feeling silly. "I'm Alison Grey."

"Yes, I know," the dark-haired guy replied with a grin. "I'm Antonio Luís Mendoza. Everyone calls me Tony."

"You new at Chandler?"

"New this year, yes," Tony replied, with a twinkle lighting his dark brown eyes. "Dr. Dorn has done me a great favor. I've been wanting to meet you."

"Why?" Alison asked, immediately suspicious.

Tony was kept from a reply by the sharp rap of Dr. Dorn's ruler. "Class, may I have your attention. I have prepared a syllabus for the next six weeks. Amy, will you pass these out while I explain? All of your equipment will be checked out to you and your lab partner. You are responsible for each piece. We will run experiments each day in class. In addition, I shall expect a ten-page paper from each unit on one of the subjects listed in your syllabus. I want you to co-author this paper. Our library has books on reserve to assist you. Use your study halls wisely."

During lab class Alison sneaked looks at her new partner. In profile his features were sharp. His black curly hair came down in a widow's peak on his forehead. She could see the faint shadow of a beard on his bronze face, making him look older than the average guy at school.

The bell rang and the students scrambled to get their things together. Someone asked Alison a question and when she turned back around, Tony was going out the door. He moved with the grace of an athlete.

"Boy, are you lucky," Dana said as they went out. "Every girl in here wanted Tony for a partner."

"Why?"

"Are you blind? Because he's cute, not to mention smart. Every senior girl has her cap set for him. Better not poach, little junior."

Oh, damn! Not another one, Alison thought. "Well, you can tell all those hungry seniors he's safe. I have no caps or any other item of clothing set for Señor Mendoza!"

"Sure, Alison," Dana said in a hurt voice. "I was only teasing." She hurried down the hall to catch up with her friends.

Alison felt like kicking herself. She'd done it again! Dana was only being friendly and she'd snapped her head off. Unreasonably, she blamed her new partner. Guys were nothing but trouble.

After dinner she phoned Deek. Mrs. Thomas answered, and after a slight hesitation called Deek. "I'll take it upstairs," she heard Deek say.

"Hi, Alison," Deek said breathlessly, then waited for the click of the downstairs phone. "Whew! Talk about perfect timing."

"What's wrong?"

"Everything! I'm in real trouble. You just interrupted a major discussion of my very dim future," Deek replied. "My grades were awful. I got a D in algebra. My folks are upset. So am I, for that matter."

"You can pull it up. You're not a D student."

"I know it. You know it. And my parents know it. That's why they're upset. They say it's because I'm doing too much. The awful thing is, they're right!"

"Maybe you should give up something."

"That's what they say. I don't want to. I like

everything I'm doing. And to make matters worse, Marilyn just asked me to be the girls' sports reporter for the yearbook.''

"I thought Tracy Ellmore was.''

"She was. Her father was transferred to D.C. She's leaving in two weeks.''

"Why doesn't Marilyn do it? She's sports editor.''

"Alison, you know Marilyn's a space case when it comes to sports. She doesn't know a basketball from a hockey puck. The only reason she has the job is because she's good at grammar.''

"It doesn't hurt that her best friend, Carol, is editor-in-chief. Why don't you just say no?''

"I can't,'' wailed Deek. "You know how Marilyn is. Besides, she asked me as one Maiden to another.''

"Tell her your folks won't let you, then.''

"It sounds so babyish to say that. Even though it might be true,'' Deek said dispiritedly. "They may even make me drop something else if my grades don't improve.''

"I'll be glad to help if you can find the time.''

"Hey, that would be radical! Especially with algebra. Say, how did A.L.S. go?''

"I was lucky. I pulled a B for the six weeks. I'm never going to do that again. Goof off, I mean. It takes too much work to catch up.''

"Congratulations! I'm glad I'm not in one of Dr. Dorn's classes. What's lower than an F?''

"Twenty other letters in the alphabet.''

"Oh, pooh! You know what I mean, Alison Grey. So what else is new?''

"I have a new lab partner. A guy named Tony Mendoza. Know him?"

"Don't I wish! I've seen him around but never met him. He's a mystery guy."

"What does that mean?"

"Well, he's the subject at the lunch table, the locker room, and the club meetings. Yet no one knows very much to talk about," Deek answered, stopping provocatively.

"Go on, Deek. You know you're dying to tell me."

Deek giggled. "Okay, but it isn't much. He lives with his uncle, who is head of the language department out at Sexton College. Tony's smart, handsome, and very polite, and doesn't seem interested in girls. End of report."

"You're right. That isn't much."

"Marilyn thinks he's queer."

"Queer queer, or queer odd? And why?" Alison asked.

"Queer gay. Because she asked him to a party one night and he politely refused the sex queen of Chandler High."

"That doesn't make him gay. Just smart."

"Other girls have had the same polite turndown," Deek warned.

"Not to fear. He's my lab partner, nothing else."

"You're safe there. He's the leading senior in class rank. Pushed Carol Hardy from first place, I hear."

"I like him better all the time."

"Alison, I want to talk with you about Carol—" Deek began.

"Not now," interrupted Alison. "I just finished my dinner. Besides, I have homework. You want to come over and study?"

"I wish I could. I have plenty to do. But I have a meeting at seven-thirty. I'd better fly. Can I take a rain check?"

"Sure," Alison replied and hung up.

She went back to her room and put on some old Simon and Garfunkel tapes. She felt sad. Once upon a time Deek would have been over in a flash. Selfishly, she wished Deek's parents would make her drop out of Athena's Maidens. It was hard to be someone's best friend when you hardly ever saw her, didn't run in the same crowd, or take part in the same activities. She and Deek were drifting apart. Going their separate ways. Even if they didn't want to. Where did that leave her?

The conversation with Dr. Dorn came back to Alison with amazing clarity. She hadn't had time to think about it before, as she'd promised. There were actually other people attending Chandler High besides the Greeks! Maybe she hadn't given anyone a chance to be her friend. But how did she go about changing?

Chapter Eight

A loud crash followed by a soft "Damn!" caused Alison to turn and glance over her shoulder. The contents of a locker were scattered all over the hall.

Elizabeth Allen, a shy, quiet senior, stood looking down at the mess, a flush of anger on her pale cheeks.

Instead of going on about her business, Alison turned and walked back. "What happened?"

"The shelf broke! Wouldn't you know it would happen when I had my art stuff on it?"

"I'll get some paper towels from the restroom. It's only watercolor, so it'll wipe up."

"Thanks," Elizabeth replied, stooping to retrieve her notebooks from the spreading paint.

It took only a few minutes to get the mess cleared away. "I hope this doesn't make you late to class," Elizabeth said. "Thanks for the help."

"You're welcome. I was only going to lunch."

"So was I. We've still got time to partake of the gourmet fare if we hurry."

"Do we really want to?"

"I'm game if you are," Elizabeth said as they

hurried to the cafeteria. "There's a place over in the corner."

"What is this stuff?" Alison asked as they set their trays down.

"They said it was a Mexican casserole," Elizabeth answered, wrinkling her delicate nose.

"Probably a new name for leftovers. But why blame the Mexicans?"

Elizabeth took a tiny forkful. "It's not so bad," she pronounced. "Better than the usual."

"Can my digestive system quote you on that?" Alison asked. It felt good to have company at lunch. Much better than eating alone or reading while you ate.

Elizabeth proved to be an interesting companion. Poetry and art were her interests, and horses were her passion. Next fall she planned to enter Hollins College, where she could indulge in all three. Alison was sorry when lunch was finished.

"See you tomorrow?" Elizabeth asked as they parted.

"Same time, same place—without the mess," Alison replied. She gathered her books and hurried to A.L.S.

Margie Wampler stopped her in the hall. "Can I borrow your English class notes? I had a dental appointment and missed class."

"Sure," Alison said, rummaging through her notebooks.

"Did you know Tilly took your place in the Maidens?" Margie asked, rather casually.

"No. I couldn't care less who joined."

"Me either! Thanks for the notes. I'll meet you

here after school and give them back. Maybe we could go to Lucky's for a Coke?'' Margie said tentatively.

''Sure. I don't have swim practice today. Miss Stevens is attending a district coaches' meeting,'' Alison said with sudden compassion. Margie had lost her best friend just as she had. Tilly and Deek were too busy to go for Cokes after school now.

The delay almost made Alison late. The tardy bell rang just as she walked in the door. She hurried to her seat and found Tony smiling at her with a devastating, white-toothed grin.

He rose and pulled out her chair. That brought giggles from the rest of the class and a flush to Alison's face. It didn't seem to bother Tony in the least.

Dr. Dorn cleared her throat for attention and got it. She lectured briskly for thirty minutes.

Alison kept her eyes glued on Dr. Dorn or her notebook. But she could occasionally feel Tony's eyes on her. It rattled her, but she hoped it didn't show.

After the lecture, everyone lined up to check out the lab equipment. There was no time for casual conversation as they set up. Much to her surprise, she and Tony worked very well together. They finished the classification of their slides before the rest of the class and quietly put away their equipment.

''Have you thought about a topic for our paper yet?'' Tony whispered.

''Not really. Which one interests you?''

''How about number four?''

Pleased, Alison whispered back, "That was on my list, too."

The first bell rang and everyone began rushing around, cleaning up. Tony gathered his books hurriedly. "We have a problem, Alison. I don't have a study hall."

"Neither do I."

"Well," Tony said, flashing that smile again, "we'll have to work something out tomorrow."

Before Alison could reply, he was out the door. I won't, Alison told herself, I simply *will not* get interested in another flashy, good-looking guy! Señor Mendoza is my lab partner. That's all. Period.

Margie was waiting in the hall. They went to Lucky's and, much to Alison's surprise, it was as if all those weeks of self-imposed exile had never happened.

Afterward, Alison walked home through the park, enjoying the autumn trees that were just beginning to change colors. School was becoming more bearable every day. There were other interesting people at Chandler. And no one seemed to hate her now. Maybe they never had. Not all of them, anyway. Could it have been only her attitude? Her imagination? No! There was still someone who hated her enough to spread rumors about her. She knew who that was! Still, if she could continue to avoid Carol, school might not be totally miserable. It was a big school. It shouldn't be too difficult if she kept a low profile and avoided her enemy.

With rising spirits, Alison kicked through the wine and maroon leaves cluttering her driveway.

Once again, the house seemed to welcome her.

* * *

Tony drummed his long, slender fingers on the lab table. "I've been thinking about when we could do our research," he said while Dr. Dorn was momentarily out of class. "We could use the college library."

"I hadn't thought of that," Alison admitted. "I've never used it, but I know some of the other kids do."

"The problem is," Tony continued, "I'm on a rather tight schedule. I can meet you only on Friday nights, Saturday afternoons, or anytime Sunday."

Another mystery! Tony wasn't involved in any school activities. She'd quietly asked around. "I'm free this Friday."

"Good. I was afraid you'd have another date," Tony said, giving her one of his dazzling smiles. Then, seeing the look on Alison's face, he added, "I wanted us to get started on this project immediately. Dr. Dorn sets high standards for a high school teacher."

"Yes, she does," Alison agreed, frowning. Another date? What did that mean? This was schoolwork!

"Is something wrong, Alison? Are you having trouble with your microscope?" Dr. Dorn asked from the front of the room.

"No, Dr. Dorn. I was just thinking through a problem. Nothing I can't handle."

Dr. Dorn nodded and smiled.

Alison wasn't as sure of herself as she sounded.

Since Tony wasn't interested in other girls at Chandler, what was his interest in her?

When Tony said, "How about seven-thirty?" Alison answered shortly, "Fine, I'll meet you at the front desk in the library." She didn't want him picking her up as if it were a date.

"This is your big chance," Deek said when Alison told her about the work session.

"What does that mean?" Alison snapped.

"Don't have a cow, man! I mean you'll have a chance to find out about this mystery dude. You owe it to your classmates."

"Put a sock in it, Deek!"

When Margie made the same request, Alison knew she was hooked.

Friday night finally came. She changed outfits three times. She couldn't decide whether to dress like a typical college student in jeans or wear her usual skirt and sweater. Since she really didn't care for jeans unless she was grubbing around, she chose her heather skirt and matching sweater.

Peering through the glass doors of the Sexton library, Alison found her heart thumping unpleasantly and was annoyed with herself. Several students walked past her dressed in jeans, making her feel overdressed and conspicuous. She peeked through the doors again. Tony was at the desk, talking to someone. He looked totally at ease, dressed in his usual slacks and button-down shirt. I don't think I've ever seen him in jeans, Alison thought as she opened the door.

Tony waved her over. "Hi, Alison," he said with a warm welcome in his voice. "This is Miss

Meeks. She says we may use Conference Room B since we might need to talk.''

Alison said hello and followed Tony through the stacks.

After two hours of intensive work and discussion, Tony stretched and gave her a satisfied smile. ''I think we deserve a reward for our efforts. How about a burger and fries at the snack bar?''

''Sounds good to me,'' Alison replied, shutting her book and rubbing the back of her neck. ''Lead the way.''

The snack bar was crowded but they found a table in the corner. Tony seemed right at home. Some people even greeted him by name. Alison drew a few admiring looks, which she pretended not to notice.

After they were served, Alison took the plunge. ''Well, I've completed one assignment. Now for number two.''

Tony raised one thick eyebrow. ''What else is on your agenda tonight? Do you have to leave now?''

''Oh, no. I have to stay. My second task is to find out more about you. You're quite the mystery man, you know.''

Tony's eyes twinkled mischievously. ''Far be it from me to prevent a pretty lady from accomplishing her assignment. You'll find, I'm afraid, nothing so mysterious. Ask away.''

''Right,'' Alison said in the same teasing tone. ''Who are you? Why are you living here? Where do you disappear to every day? What are your interests besides school? What are your favorite foods, songs, sports, colors?''

"Let's start with the easy ones. My favorite color is blue—the shade of your sweater. My favorite food is a Spanish bouillabaisse. I don't have a favorite song. Soccer is my favorite sport."

"Those were the easy ones!"

"The other ones aren't difficult. I'm afraid once you solve the mystery, I will no longer be of interest."

"Try me," Alison challenged.

Tony assumed a lecturing posture. "I am Antonio Luís Mendoza. Age eighteen. A dual citizen of Spain and the United States. Son of a Spanish ambassador and an American mother, both deceased. I have lived in four countries and attended seven schools, most of them private. I live now with my uncle, Dr. Mendoza, in order to finish my high school education. I plan to enter the University of Virginia next fall to study microbiology. I work three days a week in Gentry Photography Studios. That's where I go after school. I take a class two nights a week here at Sexton. My outside interests are photography and soccer. Since Chandler doesn't have a soccer team, I sub for Sexton's."

"Sounds pretty interesting to me."

"Turnabout is fair play, I hear. Tell me about yourself."

"My story's pretty dull."

"Try me," Tony said, repeating her challenge.

Alison grinned. "Okay. My name is Alison Elaine Grey. Age sixteen and a half. American citizen. In fact, my family has lived in this town for three generations. Youngest of the three daughters of James and Elaine Grey. I'm dying to finish high school and go to college, but I don't know where or what I want to study. My outside interests are reading and swimming. I swim on the varsity team for Chandler.''

''I find you very interesting,'' Tony said, gazing directly into her eyes. ''In fact, I would like to get to know you better.''

Alison retreated immediately. ''I'm sure we'll get better acquainted working on this project.'' Glancing at her watch, she said, ''Oh, goodness. It's getting late. I'd better get home.''

Tony looked disappointed, but rose as she did. ''I'll walk you to your car. I'm sorry I couldn't offer to pick you up. I don't have a car.''

''I don't, either. Mom let me borrow hers,'' Alison said quickly. She was glad to escape anything more personal with Tony.

On the way home she tried to analyze her feelings. Why did Tony frighten her? He and Nic were as different as night and day. It wasn't just their coloring, either. Tony was sure of himself without being cocky. Although Nic would never have liked a girl who wasn't pretty, Tony wouldn't like a girl who was dumb. One thing for sure, Tony wasn't gay. She didn't know how she knew, but she was positive of this. So what was her hang-up? Why had she cut Tony short?

Because, she thought grimly, I was wrong before. I don't want to make the same mistake again. My track record's pretty lousy.

Chapter
Nine

On Monday Dr. Dorn approved their project. They were to collect smears from supposedly clean places, grow the cultures on agar-agar, and classify each bacterium found. Tony and Alison set to work making sterile petri dishes, dividing the list of sites.

Alison's other classes were going well. Even so, homework didn't take up all of her time. There were parties, dances, and other events to which she wasn't invited. Deek came over several times to get help with her algebra. And Alison and Margie went to a couple of movies. But there were still large gaps to be filled.

One Friday as she walked out of English class, Fred Taylor called out, "Hey, wait up, Alison."

She turned around, smiling. She'd known Fred since first grade and had, perhaps, spoken two dozen words to him in all that time. To say Fred was quiet was an understatement.

"Wouldjaliketogotoamovie?"

"Sure, Fred. What's playing?" Alison said slowly, allowing him to catch his breath.

"There's a Woody Allen movie at the Capri. I—

I can't remember the title," Fred stammered. "We could go over to Rippley if you don't like that."

"I like Woody Allen."

"Me, too. Pick you up at—uh—eight-thirty?"

"Tonight at eight-thirty," Alison confirmed.

"I meant tomorrow," Fred said, blushing to the roots of his blond hair.

"I'll be ready," Alison said and went off to join Elizabeth for lunch.

During A.L.S. Tony leaned over and whispered, "I hear there's a Woody Allen movie playing. Would you like to go tomorrow night?"

Alison felt like screaming. Why now? She'd been sitting home, counting the flowers in her wallpaper for weeks. Now she had two offers. "Sorry, I already have a date," she whispered.

The disappointed look on Tony's face made her heart ache. An idea that had been in the back of her mind all week pushed forward. Before she could change her mind, she tore off a slip of paper and wrote Tony a note: Wait a minute after class. I have a great idea.

Tony read the note and nodded.

As soon as the bell rang, Alison said, "Have you been up on the Blue Ridge Parkway, Tony?"

"No. Uncle promised we would go, but we never seem to get the time."

"How about us going up there on Sunday? There's a place called Holly Springs that claims to have the purest water in the world. We could test it for our project."

"And I could take photographs," Tony said enthusiastically.

"I'll make a picnic."

"Oh, no! I'll make the picnic," Tony insisted.

"Okay, it's a deal. What time?"

"Would ten o'clock be too early?"

"Not for me. We can hike before we eat," Alison said. "Hey, I just remembered. I don't know where you live."

"At the faculty center. Apartment two-twenty. I'll be out front, though," Tony called as he dashed for the door. "I'm going to miss my bus."

Saturday night was strange. They both enjoyed the funny movie, but afterward was awkward. Alison didn't know what Fred was interested in, and he wasn't much help. He answered her in one or two words, then the conversation was over. After a short visit to Lucky's, Fred drove her home.

"I enjoyed the movie, Fred," Alison said at her door.

"Yeah, Allen's pretty funny," Fred said for the tenth time. "Well, see you in English Monday."

"Thanks for a nice evening."

"Welcome," he replied and stumbled down the last two steps.

Alison didn't know whether to laugh or cry. She wished she'd been able to put Fred at ease. He really was a nice guy even if he did behave like a terrified rabbit around girls.

"Is that you, Alison?" her mother called.

"Yes, Mother."

"How was the movie?"

"The movie was funny. My date was strange. Were you waiting up for me?"

"No, dear. Your father. His plane was due at eleven-thirty, so he should be here any moment."

"Oh, yeah. I forgot. Tell him hi for me. I've got to get some sleep if I'm going to get up early."

"Early on a Sunday morning? Will wonders never cease!"

"I'm taking Tony up on the parkway, remember? You said I could borrow your car. It's for a school project."

"I remember. Just don't wake your father. He's had a long, hard week. I don't even think we'll go to church."

"Will wonders never cease!" Alison said teasingly. "Okay, I'll be as quiet as a mouse." She bounded upstairs with a trace of the old spring in her step, quiet Fred already forgotten.

As Alison drove around the block looking for a parking place, she saw Tony come out of the faculty center, dressed in jeans and a sweater, carrying a backpack. The jeans fitted him like a glove, emphasizing his slender hips. She tooted the horn and he came hurrying toward her.

"Punctual as usual, I see," he said, slipping in and easing the backpack from his shoulders.

"Couldn't waste a minute of a day like this," Alison said, waving her hand at the crystal-blue sky. "Did you pack everything in that one knapsack?"

"Certainly. Lunch, petri dishes, swab, catch bottle, camera, film, and first-aid supplies. You are talking to an experienced hiker—not a greenhorn."

"I'm impressed."

Tony was impressed with the Blue Ridge Parkway. He took two rolls of film before they stopped to eat at Holly Springs.

Conversation flowed between them like a river. It surprised Alison that two people from such different backgrounds could hold so many of the same opinions and share so many interests. Talking with Tony was as easy as talking with Fred had been difficult.

As they sat side by side on a rocky hillside, overlooking a multihued valley below, Alison said, "I'm curious, Tony. On that first day as my lab partner, why did you say you'd been wanting to meet me?"

"Because it was true."

"You could have introduced yourself anytime."

"That's not the way it's done in Spain."

"You mean we needed a formal introduction?"

"No," Tony replied, choosing his words carefully. "It was a matter of timing. You had your mind on other matters."

Alison felt the heat rise on her face. Somehow she'd hoped Tony hadn't heard the ugly gossip. "You heard the rumors about Nic and me?"

Tony nodded. "Everyone felt duty bound to inform me of this brouhaha. Your courage in the face of those rumors was what first attracted me."

"Courage? I was a basket case! A total zombie."

"Not in the beginning. You carried yourself like a queen, ignoring those guttersnipes. Later you went into a slump and had me worried."

"You and Dr. Dorn. I almost washed out of A.L.S."

"Ah, but you didn't! The way you came back and aced the exam—that morning the *duende* was upon you, Alison!"

"The what?"

"*Duende*," Tony said, smiling. "*Duende* is a Spanish term that's hard to define. It means an inner force—a mysterious power—that shines out and makes one capable of doing the impossible with ease. When I saw you on exam morning, I knew you'd do well."

"I wish you'd told me. I suffered agony all weekend."

"You forget, I didn't know you then. I couldn't call up a perfect stranger and say, 'Hey, you passed your exam. I know because the *duende* was upon you.' You would have thought me mad."

"Yes, I would have," Alison said, laughing. "I must really have been out of it not to notice you watching me."

Tony's eyes twinkled. "Girl watching is a Spanish art form. Now I think I must be more circumspect."

A breeze rippled through her hair, blowing wisps of dark curls around her face. Alison pulled a ribbon from her pocket and started to tie her hair in a ponytail.

"Please! Don't tie it back," Tony said, catching her hand.

"Okay." For some unknown reason, she blushed and looked away.

Tony began snapping pictures. "I'm very glad you brought me up here, Alison. I would have missed all of this if I'd stayed in Spain."

"Why did you come over here?"

A veil of sadness dropped over Tony's face. It made him look as young and vulnerable as a small boy.

"That was rude," Alison said quickly. "I didn't mean to pry."

"I think friends should know about each other," Tony said, taking a deep breath. "When my parents were killed in a plane crash two years ago, I went into a depression. We were very close, my parents and I. I dropped out of school. Went to live with my father's sister, *tía* Luisa, and did nothing. You see, I blamed myself for my parents' death."

"Why?"

"Because we always vacationed together until that summer. I begged off. I was too old to be accompanying my parents. My friend Carlos and I wanted to go camping and photographing in the Basque country, as befitted young men of our age. My parents reluctantly agreed and flew off to the south of France. To make a long story short, while hiking I fell and fractured my skull. My parents chartered a small plane and flew to be at my side. The plane crashed, killing all three—*mamá*, *papá*, and the pilot. After I recovered, life seemed pointless. I blamed my selfishness for their deaths. I would still be in Spain, doing nothing, if it had not been for Uncle Alfredo. He came and went on a grand rampage!"

Alison was unable to picture Tony as a morose layabout. But she saw the pain that filled his dark eyes with unshed tears and instinctively reached out to comfort him. Her warm hand clasped Tony's cool one. The contact brought a shadow of a smile to Tony's lips.

"No one resists Uncle Alfredo when he goes on a rampage. He is truly awesome. He said I was wasting my life. He raged and stormed like an angry bull. 'A Mendoza does not act in this manner. You are dishonoring your family name. Your parents would be ashamed!' He got through to me," Tony said, raking a hand through his hair. "The Spanish have a saying, 'It is hard to sleep with a dog yapping at your heels.' So I woke up and here I am."

"I'm glad," Alison said, withdrawing her hand. The warmth had become altogether too much.

"So am I. Sleeping is good. But not for a lifetime."

"Right. You wouldn't want to be another Rip Van Winkle," Alison said lightly.

"Who is this Rip Vanderwinkle?"

"Van Winkle. A character in American literature. Your education has been sadly neglected if you don't know him."

"Perhaps you will lend me a book about this man?"

"Sure," Alison replied. The dangerous moment was past now, and she intended to keep things casual from here on. "We can't have you running off to UVA without knowing old Rip."

"There's a lot that I don't know that I'd like to know," Tony said, reaching for her hand again.

Alison jumped to her feet. "Well, I can tell you one thing. If we plan to do any more hiking we'd

better get our sample of spring water and get moving.''

"I think we have plenty of time," Tony said,
smiling at her. But he followed her down to the
little spring nestled between the two hills.

Chapter
Ten

Being the odd one out wasn't so bad, Alison thought as she and Elizabeth went their separate ways after lunch. Dr. Dorn was right. There were lots of friendly people at Chandler. All she'd had to do was bend a little—not be so aloof—and things went pretty smoothly. Sure, there were a few glitches. Rob and Carol, to name two. Rob she ignored. Carol she avoided, walking away every time Carol approached her. So far, no problems this six weeks.

"You win the lottery or something?" Tony asked while they were putting their microscope in the storeroom.

"No. Why?"

"You seem exceptionally happy today."

"I think I'm finally getting my act together."

"What act?" Tony asked, looking puzzled.

His face looked so funny Alison laughed out loud. Heads turned. Dr. Dorn looked toward the supply room, frowning. "It means," Alison whispered, "I've come out of my depression just like you did. Life doesn't feel so hopeless anymore."

"That *is* good! Let's celebrate. Are you free Saturday?"

"I have swim practice in the morning."

"Oh, I forgot. I have a soccer game in the afternoon. Could we meet afterward?"

"How about if I come see you play?"

"I only get in the game if we're ahead," Tony warned, but he looked pleased. "We could celebrate afterward. How does a double chocolate sundae sound?"

"Delicious and fattening."

Tony's eyes flicked over her appreciatively. "You have nothing to worry about, Alison."

She felt heat rising in her face. "What time and where?"

"Miles Stadium. One-thirty. I'll meet you at the west gate when it's over. Okay?"

"Okay."

"It's been a long time since anyone watched me play," Tony said, smiling. "Uncle doesn't like soccer."

"I'll cheer my head off," Alison promised, then giggled. "Probably at the wrong time. I don't know the game very well."

"Just knowing you're there will be enough to inspire me."

Soccer was fast paced and exciting, Alison discovered, as she sat with the small crowd in the large stadium. Tony played with intensity when he finally got in the game. She felt an unexpected surge of pride when the people around her praised his skill.

Lucky's sundaes were humongous, gooey, and

delicious. The conversation and company were even better. She and Tony never seemed to run out of things to discuss. She was disappointed when Tony looked at his watch and said, "I'm sorry, Alison, but we'd better go. I got called in to work the five-to-ten shift at Gentry's and it's four-thirty."

"You'll never make it," Alison said, standing up quickly.

"No sweat. I'll walk you home and catch a bus."

"You can walk me as far as Patrick Henry and Jefferson," Alison said firmly. "There's a bus stop there, and I'm perfectly capable of getting the rest of the way home on my own."

"You are capable of doing most things on your own, Alison," Tony said. "But where I come from, this is not the polite thing to do."

"It's what works," Alison said. "Get a move on, Antonio."

Monday morning Tony was waiting at her locker. "Thanks to you, I made it to work with two minutes to spare," he said.

"Told you the American way works," Alison said, laughing.

Tony walked her to homeroom, and somehow during the whole week he managed to turn up and walk with her to most of her classes.

"You're a matched set," Deek teased one morning after Tony had left.

"What does that mean?" Alison asked, blushing.

"Oh, pooh! Don't play dumb, Alison Grey. Don't try to deny you and Tony have a thing going.

Why, you two don't know the rest of us exist when you walk down the hall.''

"Tony's a good friend. That's all. It's a purely platonic relationship," Alison sputtered.

"Yeah, and I'm Phi Beta Kappa material," Deek said, laughing and dancing away before Alison could punch her.

Alison was forced to reevaluate the relationship on Saturday. When she won the 200-meter freestyle at the district meet, Tony was the first person to congratulate her.

He hugged her, wet suit and all. "You swim like a *sirena*—a mermaid!"

It wasn't his words, but the electricity she felt with his arms around her. "You're all wet," she said shakily.

"So are you," Tony said, stepping back. But his eyes let her know he'd felt the same wild current.

Fortunately—or unfortunately—she was swept away by her happy, cheering teammates. They'd won, and victory was sweet. It made the long hours of practice, the chlorine-dry skin, and the daily shampoos worthwhile.

In the locker room Nancy Miller clapped Alison on the back. "Awesome, Grey. Totally awesome."

"You, too, Miller."

"Everyone performed well," Miss Stevens said. "I'm very proud of you."

Sixteen faces glowed with happiness.

When she was going home after the meet, Alison's thoughts turned to Tony. He was important to her. And in spite of her reservations, she was becoming involved. Her emotions weren't to be trusted, though! Look how she'd behaved with Nic. She needed to know Tony better—outside of school and sports. Somewhere safe . . .

"Do we have anything special on tomorrow?" she asked at dinner that evening.

"I don't think so. Why?" Mrs. Grey asked.

"I thought maybe I could invite Tony over for dinner. He probably gets tired of his uncle's cooking. Besides, we need to finish our A.L.S. report."

"That would be nice. Why don't you do that? You'll be here, won't you, James?"

"I'll be here," Mr. Grey said with a twinkle in his eyes. "I wouldn't want to miss meeting this fellow Alison quotes all the time."

"I do not!"

"Sure you do. You say, 'Tony says' at least ten times every meal."

"Now, James . . ." Mrs. Grey cautioned.

Alison only laughed at her father's teasing. "You just wait till you meet Tony. You'll see why. He's not like most guys around here."

Despite her brave words, Alison had a few moments of unease before Tony arrived. What if her folks hated him? After all, he wasn't a Virginian, not even 100 percent American. She knew how her mother felt about old Virginia families. And her father hadn't liked Ellen's husband at first. What would she do if things got awkward?

Her fears proved groundless. Tony charmed them both. With her mother, he was sincerely complimentary about the house and the excellent food. And while Alison and her mother cleared the table,

Tony and her father had a lively discussion about the European Community.

After they finished their report and Tony left, Mr. Grey began teasing Alison. "Are you sure he's only eighteen? He seems more mature than any of the young men who come to work for me. I'll bet he's really about thirty-something."

"You just don't think anyone under thirty has any sense," countered Alison.

"Well, I thought he was delightful!" Mrs. Grey said stoutly. "You two make—good lab partners, I suppose."

Alison laughed at her mother's quick recovery. "Thanks for having such a great dinner."

Mrs. Grey beamed. "You must invite Tony back again soon. I'll fix some of my deviled crab cakes. I'll bet he'd like those."

"I'm sure he would," Alison said, giving her a quick hug.

But before she had a chance to ask Tony back, he issued an invitation of his own. "Uncle Alfredo wants to reciprocate," he explained. "I'm sure it won't be as good as your mother's cooking, but Uncle makes excellent Spanish dishes."

"I'd love to come. I'd like to try authentic Spanish food."

"Good. Sunday at eight. I'll pick you up. Uncle says I may borrow his car for the event."

"I didn't know he had a car," Alison said in amazement.

"Oh, yes. But it's only used for special occasions," Tony replied, laughing. "It's a silver Mercedes. His pride and joy."

Tony picked her up promptly at eight. The Mercedes was a beautiful car with seats of special hand-tooled black leather. Alison felt like a VIP in it. Tony drove very carefully and expertly.

Dr. Mendoza met them at the door of the faculty center. After one quick glance to see if his car had survived the hazardous trip, he welcomed Alison courteously and led the way to the apartment.

He was not what Alison expected. She had pictured him as an older version of Tony. He was not. Dr. Mendoza was a large, broad-chested man with a full, neatly trimmed black beard. He moved quickly on tiny feet that seemed too small to support his heavy frame. His dark, curly hair and his brown eyes were like Tony's, except that Dr. Mendoza's hair was sprinkled with gray and his eyes seemed to bore right through you.

The dinner was delicious. Everything was Spanish, even the table wine, which Alison sipped cautiously. Normally, she didn't care for wine, but this had a delicate fruity taste and a heavenly bouquet.

Dr. Mendoza was a gracious host and a good conversationalist. But underneath the politeness, Alison felt he was judging her. It was nothing she could put her finger on, but it made her slightly uncomfortable.

After dinner Tony showed her samples of his photography. The pictures were beautiful, both in composition and color.

"You have a real talent, Tony! An eye for what is interesting as well as beautiful," Alison said, examining a picture of a child at a Spanish festival.

"Thank you," Tony said with honest pride. Then

he handed her a picture of herself taken on the parkway.

Against a backdrop of autumn reds and golds, Alison sat on a flat rock, her hair windblown, smiling into the camera. She looked like a fashion model. "Tony, this is great! I don't even look like myself!"

"That is the way you look," Tony replied, offended. "The camera never lies."

"The heck it doesn't! Have you seen my driver's license?"

"You had a bad photographer. That's the only possible explanation."

"Would you teach me how to take good pictures? There've been so many times I've wished I could."

"Sure. I'd like that, if you're interested."

Dr. Mendoza called them back into the living room for after-dinner espresso. Alison found it too bitter for her taste, but drank it anyway. Dr. Mendoza continued his probing questions. But he did seem a little friendlier than he had at first. However, Alison was glad when it was time to go.

Tony drove her home. They made polite conversation until he pulled into the driveway. "What's the matter, Alison?" he asked, turning off the ignition and facing her.

She started to say, "Nothing." Instead, she blurted out the truth. "I don't think your uncle likes me very much."

Tony sighed in exasperation. "I might have known you'd sense something!" he said, running his fingers through his hair. "Please let me explain. I don't want you to think ill of my uncle. He has been very good to me—taking me into his home, feeding, clothing, and educating me. I don't come into my inheritance until I'm twenty-five. Then I will repay him.''

"What does this have to do with me?''

"I'm getting to that. Hang on. Even with all of his kindness, Uncle is a very opinionated man. He thinks he's my *niñera*—my nursemaid. He holds many Old World values. He is appalled at the behavior of today's young people and its results. He is determined to save me from it.''

"From what?''

"From the loose morality of today's youth, Uncle says. You know, public displays of affection, students dropping out of school, getting married early, children having children.''

"I see,'' Alison said coldly. "So your uncle thinks I would lead you to destruction.''

"No, he panicked because he didn't know you. For the first time, I was spending a lot of time with a girl about whom he knew nothing. I was afraid to ask you to meet Uncle until I knew you better. That made him even more suspicious, especially when he could see we were becoming seriously involved.''

"Who says we are?''

"I do,'' Tony said quietly. "I like you very much, Alison.'' He leaned over and kissed her.

The kiss was soft and tasted faintly of wine. Though gentle, it started a tingle that went from Alison's lips to her toes.

"Will you try to forgive Uncle's behavior? It's

very important to me that you do," Tony said earnestly.

"Yes," Alison replied, remembering how she'd felt about her parents' opinion. She sighed. "He isn't the only one who has doubts about this relationship."

"I know," Tony said, finding her lips again.

When Alison opened her eyes the world stopped spinning. The night was filled with a zillion stars. She felt as if she were floating among them without a care in the world. "I'd better go," she said huskily. "Uncle Alfredo will be worried—about his car and his nephew."

"I shall return both in very good condition."

"Thanks for a super evening," Alison said when they reached her door.

"My pleasure." Tony kissed her briefly and ran lightly down the steps.

Alison watched him drive away. Her heart was fluttering very strangely. Not to worry! Tony had conquered her worst fear. She could respond—feel attraction—without Nic's ghost popping up. Tony's kiss had exorcised Nic once and for all. That alone was worth a few erratic heartbeats.

Chapter
Eleven

Alison checked her exam paper carefully, folded it, and carried it up to Dr. Dorn's desk.

"You've done excellent work these last six weeks," Dr. Dorn said softly.

"Thank you," Alison replied, "for everything."

Dr. Dorn nodded and smiled.

Tony was waiting for Alison in the hall. "That was a tough one! She gives a comprehensive exam. How did it go for you?"

"Pretty well, I think. Certainly a lot easier than the last six weeks."

"That's because you attended class this time."

"It is easier that way," Alison agreed. "I'm sorry it's over."

"Why?"

"Because we get new lab partners after Thanksgiving."

"Maybe we can talk Dr. Dorn out of switching."

"Not likely. But we'll still be in the same class. That will have to do, I guess."

"We don't see much of each other as it is," Tony complained as they walked down the hall. "I wish

I didn't have to go to New York tomorrow with Uncle! A six-day break, and we won't even get to spend one day together!''

"Thanks to you, we still have tonight," Alison said. "Are you sure you don't mind spending it at a basketball game?"

"Not if I'm with you."

"Well, I promised Deek I'd come tonight. I haven't seen her play but once this year. This is a big one—the holiday invitational."

"Sounds like fun. I've never seen a girl's basketball game. I'll pick you up at seven-thirty. Mr. Gentry's closing early for the holiday."

"I'll be ready. You'd better run or you'll miss your bus!"

Tony gave her hand a squeeze and dashed off.

Alison was glad she hadn't let him see how disappointed she was that he wouldn't be around at Thanksgiving to meet the rest of her family. She especially wanted Ellen to meet him. Yet she understood why Tony had to go. Uncle Alfredo had been planning the trip for months. They were supposed to have left tonight, but Tony had begged off.

At seven-forty-five Tony still had not come. It wasn't like him to be late. Alison phoned his house and then Gentry's. No one answered at either place.

"Mother, I promised Deek I'd be there for the tip-off. I'm going on. Will you tell Tony to meet me at the gym? Can I borrow the car? I'll be late if I don't."

"Certainly. I'm not using it. I'm sure Tony has been unavoidably detained. I'll tell him where to find you."

Alison drove quickly to the gym, lucked out on a parking space, and made it just in time for the tip-off. It was an exciting game, a seesaw battle between Grandby and Chandler for two quarters. Alison kept one eye on the action and one eye on the gym entrance.

With two seconds to go before halftime, Deek stole the ball and passed it down court to five-foot-ten Joni Mitchell. Joni dunked the ball, and Chandler led 47–45 as the buzzer sounded. The fans went wild.

Alison looked up and saw Tony come in with Carol Hardy. They were laughing and cheering! Alison's heart did a queer flip-flop and then seemed to stop altogether as Carol took Tony's arm and pulled him aside. Unable to take her eyes off of them, she watched Carol count money into Tony's outstretched hand.

A moan of anguish escaped Alison's lips as she stumbled down the bleachers and pushed her way through the gym toward the restrooms. The crowd was clotted near the doorway and she couldn't get out fast enough. She heard Tony call her name and shoved frantically.

Before she could reach the safety of the restroom, Tony caught up with her. "Alison, didn't you hear me?" he said, grabbing her arm.

"Let go of me, you—you Spanish gigolo!" she shouted, pulling free.

Tony reached out again, a puzzled, hurt look on his face.

Alison slapped him as hard as she could with the open palm of her hand. The blow echoed like a shot through the hall. People stopped and stared. "Leave me alone!" Alison cried angrily.

Tony looked at her for a long, deadly moment. His eyes glowed like black coals in his pale face. She thought fleetingly that he would strike her. Instead, he turned sharply and walked away.

Alison fled into the restroom and locked herself in a stall. The pain was so terrible it left her weak kneed. She sat down heavily and put her head between her knees to keep from fainting.

It was all a trick! Another Carol Hardy trick. Tony had accepted money for getting her to love him. How could he do that? It wasn't possible. Nic, yes. But not Tony. Yet she'd seen it with her own eyes. Everyone had seen it! Tony took money from Carol in front of everyone. This time Carol made sure that she was publicly humiliated. Why had Tony done that? Silent tears gushed from her eyes. She rocked herself back and forth to ease the pain. None of the outside noise penetrated her misery.

Finally the tears stopped. The restroom was silent. Dimly, she could hear noise from the gym. Shakily, she stood up and unlocked the door. Somehow she must get to her car without anyone seeing her. . . .

Carol Hardy leaned against the hall door, blocking her way.

"You've won," Alison said, defeated. "Let me by."

"Not this time. This time you're going to listen to me!"

"I said you'd won. Everyone saw that tonight. What more do you want?"

"I want you to listen!" Carol shouted. "Alison, I

had no idea what you were talking about when you ran out of Kanes's cabin. I only knew you were upset. I didn't know anything about a bet! I only found out about that last night. By accident. Rob got drunk at a stag party and told my boyfriend, George, about this bet he had with Nic. See, Rob bet a hundred dollars that Nic couldn't score with you. Nic had one month to do it in, and the house party was his last chance. He lost. And he wouldn't pay up. That's what the fight was about. Rob even bragged about how clever he'd been, putting the blame on you for Nic's leaving town. George said—are you listening, Alison?''

"I'm listening—but I don't understand."

"It was Rob Warren who made the bet with Nic. Not me. I didn't know anything about a bet!''

"Nic said you were in on it. He said the Handmaiden bit was your idea,'' Alison said dully.

"Well, yes, it was. But only because I thought you'd make a good Athena. I didn't make any deals. It was a rotten, stupid, vicious thing to do. Just like Nic. He's a cruel jerk. I'm truly sorry about this whole nasty business.''

"You're sorry,'' Alison repeated.

"Yes, I am. I wanted to get this straightened out over our break. Then you threw a fit because Tony talked to me.''

Alison heard Carol's words but somehow her head couldn't absorb their meaning. "You paid Tony money. I saw you.''

Patiently, Carol explained. "I paid Tony for developing some rush pictures for the yearbook. The section has to go to the printers tomorrow. Tony stayed late at Gentry's to develop them for me. I paid him for the pictures. See, here they are," Carol said, holding out an envelope of snapshots.

Slowly, as she looked at the pictures, Carol's words sank in. It was Rob. Not Carol. Rob and Nic. It made sense. Rob and Nic competed over everything. . . . "Tony!" Alison cried with anguish.

"Yeah, you really dumped on him tonight," Carol said sympathetically. "Want me to go with you and straighten things out? Tony's a nice guy. I think he'll understand."

Understand being slapped and called names in public? Alison didn't think so. "No, I'd better do it myself," she said in despair. "I don't know what came over me. I've never acted like that in my whole life."

"Maybe it's because you really care about Tony," Carol ventured. "Wash your face and go after him. Don't let this break you up."

Carol helped Alison repair some of the damage to her puffy, swollen eyes, and then led her out a side door.

"Thanks, Carol. I'm sorry I misjudged you."

"Don't waste time talking to me. Go explain to Tony."

The trip across town was awful. She caught every red light. Every car in front of her was going a nice, sedate six miles an hour! She had no idea what she was going to say to Tony. But someway, somehow she was going to make him listen to her apology!

The faculty center was almost all dark when she arrived. Most people were away for the holidays, she supposed. She parked and ran upstairs to the Mendoza apartment. The door chimes echoed in silence. She rang again. And again.

"If you're looking for Dr. Mendoza, he and his nephew left a few minutes ago for New York. I'm afraid you've missed them," an elderly man clad in a smoking jacket said, peering out of the adjoining apartment.

Alison slumped against the door. Six days for the wound to fester! It was too long. She'd lost Tony.

"Are you all right, miss?" the old man said with concern. "Would you like to come inside and rest a moment?"

"No, thanks," Alison said. She trudged back down the stairs and drove home. This time the burden was too heavy to carry alone. She found her mother and poured out the whole story.

Mrs. Grey was livid. "That's despicable! No wonder you were upset. I wish you'd told me about this."

"I couldn't tell anyone. I was too ashamed."

"Ashamed? Listen to me, Alison. You have nothing to be ashamed about! You had a right to say 'no' and have it honored. Otherwise, it's rape."

"I went to Crescent Island with Nic. I kissed him. I even enjoyed it," Alison confessed in a small voice.

"So you used poor judgment and are a normal, healthy young woman! That isn't a license for rape. The important thing is that you refused and took action. It's over now, honey."

"But it isn't!" wailed Alison. "I've hurt and humiliated Tony for no reason at all."

"Yes, you have. But if Tony's half the young man I think he is, he'll understand and forgive you."

Alison made an ineffectual swipe at the tears on

her cheeks. "I can't see Tony until Monday. That's a long time to hurt."

"Monday will come, even if every day does seem to have sixty hours in it."

"I guess you're right," Alison said, giving her mother a watery smile. "Mom, please don't tell anyone about this. Not even Dad."

"But, Alison—"

"Please, Mom. I don't want to spoil everyone's Thanksgiving. Can this be our secret?"

"All right," Mrs. Grey agreed reluctantly. "Now, go upstairs and get some sleep, or your face will give you away tomorrow."

Alison leaned over and kissed her mother's cheek. "Thanks. You've helped a lot. I couldn't hold it inside any longer."

"I'm always available," Mrs. Grey said quietly.

"I guess I've always known that even if I didn't take advantage of it," Alison said as she slipped out of the room.

Sharing helped. But not enough. Her mother's love didn't fill the void left by the absence of Tony's. Alison knew that was gone. How could it not be? She knew all too well how it felt to be humiliated.

Chapter Twelve

The holidays crept by at a snail's pace. Every time Alison thought of Tony her stomach knotted in a tight ball. In spite of her inner turmoil, she tried to put on a happy act for her family. It was good to have everyone home again—Ellen and Frank, Lisa, Gran and Gramps. The house was full of tantalizing smells and happy chatter. Her face felt stiff from keeping a smile pasted on it.

Mrs. Grey kept her word. She didn't tell anyone, as far as Alison knew. Occasionally she'd give Alison a sympathetic look, and Alison would smile back.

The time did pass. Gran and Gramps went home on Friday. Ellen and Frank left on Saturday. And Lisa was leaving today.

"We're taking Lisa to the airport early," Mrs. Grey announced Sunday afternoon. "Her plane doesn't leave till five but they're predicting snow."

"I think I'll build a fire in the fireplace before we go," Mr. Grey said. "Will you keep it going, Alison?"

"Sure. I'll sit down here and read. The house will be warm and toasty when you get back."

With heartfelt relief, Alison watched the three of them drive away. A few snowflakes wandered down as she waved goodbye to Lisa. Shivering, she went inside and curled up in her father's big chair with Stephen King's latest book. After a few pages she was thoroughly hooked. From time to time she absently put another log on the fire.

The jarring ring of the telephone nearly scared her to death.

"Lisa's plane is delayed," Mrs. Grey said when Alison answered. "We're going to wait with her, so we'll be a little late. Okay?"

"Okay. I've been so engrossed in this book, I hadn't noticed the time."

"Is it snowing there?"

"I—I don't know. I haven't looked."

"That must be a very good book! Well, I'm glad you found something to occupy your mind. We'll be home later. There's plenty to eat in the fridge."

Alison groaned. "Don't I know! I bet I've gained five pounds. Don't worry, I won't starve. Be careful driving home."

Alison went around turning on the lights. Looking through the picture window, she noticed that snow had already blanketed the ground, and the big, fat flakes were still falling. She went to the kitchen, made a turkey sandwich, and went back to the den and her book.

Sometime later, the doorbell rang.

"Dad must have forgotten his keys again," she muttered, turning the dead bolt.

The door flew open, almost knocking her over.

"Hi, Snowflake. Aren't you going to ask me in?"

Alison swallowed her panic. ''You're already in! What do you want, Nic?''

He grabbed her arm, kicked the door shut, and pushed her toward the den. ''Now is that any way for a proper hostess to behave? Where are the ice maiden's manners?''

His eyes looked weird. Was he on something? Alison forced a smile. ''Sorry. You took me by surprise. Have a seat. I'll ask mother to bring us some hot chocolate.''

Nic pulled her down on the sofa beside him, wagging a finger in her face. ''Mustn't tell lies, Snowflake. I saw your parents at the airport when I dropped Grampa off.''

''They'll be home soon.''

A giggle bubbled from Nic. ''No, they won't! The airport's socked in. We have plenty of time.''

Alison pulled her arm free. ''Go home, Nic, before you do something stupid.''

With the quickness of a snake, Nic slapped her. ''Don't call me stupid, you bitch! You owe me big time.''

Stunned, Alison didn't move for a split second. Looking at Nic's powerful body, she decided retaliation wasn't prudent. She stubbornly refused to rub her aching face. ''Why do I owe you anything?''

''Now who's being stupid?'' Nic snarled. ''You think I spent all that time and money on you for nothing?''

''Maybe I was stupid,'' Alison conceded, ''but I thought we just enjoyed each other's company.''

Nic's laughter bounced crazily around the room.

"You're too much, Alison. A real Babe in the Woods."

"Not anymore."

Nic sobered. "Yeah. I hear you're gettin' it on with some wetback."

Alison's temper flared. "You're crude, rude, and wrong, Nic Chandler! You need a brain transplant."

"What I need is some of what this Mendoza guy is getting," Nic said, pulling her to him.

The phone rang, causing both of them to jump.

"It's Deek," Alison said quickly. "She said she'd call before she came over."

Nic jerked her to her feet. "Get rid of her!" He dragged her across the room, pulling her left arm sharply behind her back. "No tricks. Act normal."

Alison choked back a scream and picked up the phone. "Hello . . . Oh, hi, Deek. Listen, can you help me with my algebra some other time? Yeah, Tony came over. . . . Mom and Dad took Lisa to the airport and . . ." Nic brought her arm higher and she gasped. "You're a pal. I knew you'd understand. See ya soon."

Nic took the receiver from her hand and placed it on the table. "No more phone calls, Snowflake. It's pay-up time." He herded her back into the den and pushed her down on the sofa.

Alison was really frightened now. She had to keep him talking! She made herself smile as Nic plopped down beside her. "You sure made Rob pay. For two weeks he looked like he had a baked potato stuck on his face."

Nic preened. "I didn't have a mark on me. And

that dumb jerk outweighs me by at least sixty pounds.''

''All brawn and no brain fits Rob to a T, doesn't it? Remember the Wilde play?''

''Yeah. He was eager to see a wild play, but not a Wilde play,'' Nic said, chuckling. ''What a jerk!''

''Hey, I heard the jerk made seven-fifty on his SAT's. Rob's going to college.''

''Sure he is. On some football scholarship. He'll flunk out unless he takes four years of basket weaving,'' Nic said, pulling her roughly into his arms. ''Let's forget about that bonehead.''

Alison struggled but Nic held her easily, pushing her backward on the sofa. He covered her face and neck with kisses while his free hand pawed under her sweatshirt.

''Stop it, Nic! Let me up!''

Surprisingly, he released her. ''You're too uptight, baby, and I'm coming down myself. I have something to make both of us happy.'' He sat up and took a small plastic bag from his shirt pocket. Dangling it before her eyes, he laughed. ''Snow for a Snowflake.''

''I don't do drugs,'' Alison said, watching with horror as he carefully poured two thin lines of white powder on the coffee table.

''Don't knock it till you've tried it, baby. This is the last of my stash. Be grateful I'm willing to share. Besides, it'll make what happens next even more fun.''

Alison looked at the poker only a few feet away. If only . . .

''Don't even think about it,'' Nic said, seizing

the back of her neck in a firm grip. "Use this straw, Snowflake. In a minute you'll feel super."

Alison blew as hard as she could. The white powder floated away like smoke.

"Bitch!" Nic screamed.

His fist slammed into her. Alison crumpled to the floor, her head striking the edge of the coffee table. The room spun. . . . Everything went black.

Chapter
Thirteen

"Alison? Alison, can you hear me? Open your eyes."

Fingers pried at her eyelids. A light shone in, sending white-hot pain skyrocketing. . . . Alison turned her head. The pain escalated a notch. "Wha . . . ?" she mumbled, fighting a wave of nausea.

"You have a concussion," a matter-of-fact voice answered.

She tried to focus her eyes. Two men in white jackets swam into view.

"Can you see me?"

"Both . . . of . . . you. Where . . . ?" She lifted her head and promptly threw up. Hands wiped her mouth. Voices floated around her. . . .

". . . Quite normal. Don't be concerned."

". . . No permanent damage?"

"Only minor concussion. We'll keep her overnight for observation."

Someone sobbed. "Why doesn't she wake up?"

"She's coming around."

Where was she? What was happening? Were those her mom's and dad's voices? Alison commanded her eyes to open. The man in the white jacket swam into focus. Shadows moved at her feet. Her face hurt! "Where?" she said through dry lips.

The man bent over her. A pencil-thin light briefly blinded her. "You're in the emergency room at the hospital, Alison. You had a bad fall. I'm Dr. Samuels. How many fingers do you see?"

"Free."

Dr. Samuels smiled. "That's good, Alison. I'll arrange a room."

The doctor moved away. Her mother took his place. Tear tracks showed plainly on her face. "Mom?"

"Your father and I are here, Alison," she said, giving Alison's hand a comforting squeeze.

A flash of memory made Alison shudder. "Nic?"

"You don't have to worry about him," her father growled. "He's in police custody!"

Her memory returned with a sickening suddenness. Nic's furious face. White powder drifting like snow. Voices . . . Sirens . . . "Help me up, please."

"Alison . . ."

"Let her try," Mr. Grey said, lifting her gently.

The room spun, then skidded to a stop. Gingerly, she felt the huge knot on her head. Her parents looked ready to pass out any moment. She tried to smile. "Hey, this feels like a baseball. How does it look?"

"Sore," her father answered. "It will look worse tomorrow. You're going to have a beautiful rainbow eye."

"It will go away shortly," Mrs. Grey said reassuringly. "No permanent damage."

"I guess it pays to have a hard head," Alison said.

"Good. You're up," Dr. Samuels said, rolling a wheelchair into the room. "Let's get you to your room, Alison. Room two-oh-four," he instructed an orderly.

In the hall a white-faced Carol Hardy and her father were waiting. Carol gasped when she saw Alison.

Alison reached for Carol's hand. "Thank you," she said with heartfelt gratitude.

A shaky smile lit Carol's face. "I thought you'd flipped out, calling me Deek. But when you asked her to help *you* with algebra, I knew something weird was going down."

"You Maidens sure stick together," Mr. Hardy said, patting Alison's shoulder. "Carol insisted I drive her over to your place, in the snow, to see what was wrong. I thought she was nuts—until we looked through the picture window and saw Nic belt you."

"I can't tell you how grateful we are, Bill," Mr. Grey said, pumping his hand. "You, too, Carol. That was some very quick thinking."

Carol smiled at Alison. "We Maidens *do* stick together."

"Glad to help," Bill Hardy replied, rubbing his massive fist. "That young hoodlum put up quite a fight. You are going to press charges, aren't you?"

"Yes!" Alison said firmly. "I've been wrong

about a lot of people, but I was right about Nic Chandler. He's dangerous.''

"I think we should get Alison to her room," Mrs. Grey said, fidgeting like a mother hen over a chick.

"We'll talk later," Carol said, touching the owl pin on her collar.

"Thanks again," Alison whispered, suddenly feeling very tired. Jovian thunder rumbled through her head.

One more ordeal awaited her. After Dr. Samuels had checked her once again, he said, "Do you feel up to talking with the police? I can put them off until morning if you don't."

Alison drew a deep breath. "Let's do it now."

"Tomorrow," Mrs. Grey said at the same time.

"I'm with Alison," Mr. Grey said, breaking the deadlock. "Let's get this over."

The two policemen were very courteous and very thorough. They took her, step by step, through the horror. Retelling it was like reliving it. It left Alison drained and shaking.

"Do you wish to press charges?" the senior officer asked formally.

"Yes, I do," Alison answered.

The officer looked at her sympathetically. "I should warn you. This could be—uh—very difficult."

Alison looked at her parents, receiving determined nods of approval. "I know, Officer. I still want to press charges."

"Good for you!"

"Gentlemen, you can see Alison at home to-

morrow if you have more questions,'' Mrs. Grey
said firmly.

Alison smiled her thanks. Her head continued to
pound ferociously.

"Close your eyes and try to rest,'' her father said
after the police left. "Your mother and I will be
right here.''

"You don't have to stay with me.''

"We want to,'' Mrs. Grey said. "Close your
eyes.''

For brief periods she dozed. A nurse came in at
regular intervals to check her vital signs. Each time
Alison saw her parents sitting in the same place,
watching over her. Silly, perhaps. But very comforting.

With orders to remain quiet for the next twenty-
four hours, Alison was allowed to go home the next
morning. At first, she complained about missing
the first day of the new six weeks. But after the
short trip home, she found she was happy to get
into bed.

"I'll bring you a lunch tray, then you can have
a nap. No visitors today,'' her mother said firmly.

"You ought to grab some Z's yourself. You and
Dad couldn't have gotten much sleep.''

"Don't worry about us. Parents are accustomed
to a 'no sleep' routine,'' Mrs. Grey assured her.

Alison ate, slept, and awoke feeling better. Except for the constantly ringing telephone, the house
was quiet. "Time to try your sea legs,'' she muttered, getting out of bed and wobbling to the bathroom.

Looking at her battered face as she brushed her

teeth brought a fresh surge of anger. What was wrong with Nic? He had everything, charm, talent, money. Why did he behave like a Neanderthal? No one had the right to do this to another person!

"You should have blown the whistle on him the first time," said the voice of her conscience. "Yelled 'date rape,' loud and clear."

"I've paid for my pride. Nic won't get off this time, no matter how nasty this gets," she promised herself. Nic wasn't even her first concern. Her heart ached for Tony. He'd be back at school, facing humiliation without explanation. The school grapevine would be busier than the downstairs phones! Poor Tony.

The persistent throbbing in her head sent her back to bed.

Carol, bless her quick-witted heart, was another problem. Unless she was badly mistaken, Carol had hinted that somehow she would be asked to rejoin Athena's Maidens, resume her rightful place with the cream at the top. Did she want that? Somehow she didn't think so. She enjoyed the freedom of choice she had now. She'd just have to find a way— a nice way—to let Carol know that.

A soft tap on her door interrupted her thoughts. "Yes?"

"I know I said no visitors," her mother said, looking in. "But this one's very persuasive."

Alison grinned. "Come on in, Deek."

Tony's head appeared. Compassion and anger fought for dominance on his face. "I told your mother it was a matter of honor."

"Tony, I'm so sorry. I want—"

"No need to explain," Tony said, coming over to the bed. "Carol hijacked me from first period and told me everything. How are you feeling?"

"Like an idiot. Boy, do I owe Carol!"

Tony sat gingerly on the side of her bed. "Carol's okay. A good friend, even if she is a little pushy. She said to tell you she and Deek had already begun damage control. Whatever that means."

"Stamping out the fires in the rumor mill," Alison explained. "Nic was a pretty popular guy here."

Anger flashed in Tony's eyes. "How could such a dog be popular?"

"Nic was like a chameleon. He could be whatever and whoever necessary to get what he wanted," Alison replied bitterly. "He fooled a lot of people. Me included."

"Forget that piece of dung!" Tony ordered. "Will you truly be all right?"

"If you forgive me I will be."

"I am compelled to forgive you," Tony said somberly. "Uncle threatened to send me back to Spain if my attitude didn't improve. Only you can guarantee that."

"You're in trouble if you must depend on a quick-tempered, hard-headed oddball like me to improve your attitude."

A smile, so full of love that it made Alison's heart race, played on Tony's face. "Spanish-Americans prefer fiery, independent women. They make life more interesting. Do you think it would hurt your poor face if I kissed it?"

"I'm sure it wouldn't."

A kiss as gentle as a butterfly wing fluttered over her face. How could anything so soft feel so wonderful?

"It will be better soon, Alison."

"It might get worse before it gets better, Tony," Alison warned. "I'm not letting Nic get away with this."

"I would expect nothing less from you. This time you will not be alone."

Alison smiled. Tony was right. Life suddenly felt very promising. It was possible to do your own thing and still have the support of others. "Give me a real kiss, please, Tony."

"Are you sure?"

"Absolutely and positively."

Teens

learn to make tough choices and the meaning of responsibility in novels by